The Bachelors

The Bachelors

DON TREMBATH

THE BLACK BELT SERIES

ORCA BOOK PUBLISHERS

National Library of Canada Cataloguing in Publication Data
Trembath, Don, 1963–
The bachelors

ISBN 1-55143-209-9

I. Title. PS8589.R392B32 2002   jC813'.54   C2002-910212-X

PZ7.T71925Ba 2002

First published in the United States, 2002

Library of Congress Catalog Card Number: 2002101879

Orca Book Publishers gratefully acknowledges the support for its publishing programs provided by the following agencies: the Government of Canada through the Book Publishing Industry Development Program (BPIDP), the Canada Council for the Arts, and the British Columbia Arts Council.

Cover illustration by Dean Griffiths
Design by Christine Toller

Printed and bound in Canada

IN CANADA:	IN THE UNITED STATES:
Orca Book Publishers	**Orca Book Publishers**
PO Box 5626, Station B	PO Box 468
Victoria, BC Canada	Custer, WA USA
V8R 6S4	98240-0468

04 03 02 • 5 4 3 2 1

To my brother, Rick, a true bachelor if there ever was one, and the kind of supporter that every writer should have.

DT

1   Jeffrey Stewart was a quiet
boy who lived with his mother, Elizabeth, and
his elderly grandparents, Edna and Sam
Anderson.

On a Tuesday night last winter, after a
day of feeling, in her own words, "like crap,"
Jeffrey's grandma checked herself into the hospital. The doctors quickly found that something was wrong with her heart. They suggested
immediate surgery and, being the battler that
she was, she went for it. They also told her
that the procedure would have to be done at a
hospital five hours away, and that she would
need a full week of care before heading back
home.

Elizabeth, an only child, and a devoted
one at that, offered to go with her mom and

to care for her during the recovery, leaving Jeffrey behind with his grandpa.

"We'll be okay, Mom," Jeffrey said, in an attempt to be reassuring.

"You'll need help," said his mother, who was only lukewarm on the idea, but could not think of anything better. She was not about to call Jeffrey's father, who had left them in the lurch a year ago.

"For what?"

"For everything."

"Grandpa will be here."

Elizabeth looked at her son and raised an eyebrow. "That's what I'm worried about the most."

They eventually reached an agreement. Jeffrey would stay home with his grandpa, but he was required to have a responsible friend stay over and help him.

At the breakfast table the next morning, Jeffrey told his mother that he had chosen his friend from karate, Charlie Cairns.

"Good God," said his mother, nearly spilling her cup of tea. "You can't invite that boy into the house."

"Why not?" said Jeffrey, his mouth full of cereal.

"Your grandfather hates him."

"He doesn't even know him."

"He doesn't have to know him. He knows of him. Now pick someone else."

"No."

"Yes."

"No."

"Jeffrey."

"What?"

"Pick someone else."

"No. It's Charlie or it's nobody."

Elizabeth sipped at her tea to steady her nerves. This was not a good time for her son to exercise his stubbornness. "Well, what about your other friend from karate?"

"Sidney?"

"Yes."

Jeffrey gave his mother a look. "Sidney's a thief, Mom."

Elizabeth rolled her eyes. "No, he's not."

"His mom is."

"That was years ago."

Jeffrey picked up a piece of toast. "All right. He drinks beer from his mom's glass every night."

"You don't know that."

"He's tried smoking cigarettes before."

"He has not."

"That's what he said."

Elizabeth stopped to think. She knew that her son had few friends. The only ones he did have were from the karate lessons he had started taking less than a year ago.

She had hoped he would have chosen the boy from up the street, Duncan McAllister, the pastor's son. But apparently Jeffrey hadn't even thought of him.

"What about Duncan McAllister?" she said.

"Who?"

She repeated the name.

"I don't know him."

"Sure you do."

"You know him better than I do."

"Well, you know who he is."

Jeffrey stopped eating for a moment. "I want somebody here I can count on, Mom. Someone I know. Someone I can trust."

"For God's sake, Jeffrey. You're not performing surgery. You're living with your grandfather for a few days."

"Hey," said Jeffrey. "It's your idea."

Elizabeth backed away.

"All right," she said, after a moment. "You can have Sidney."

Jeffrey looked at his mother. "I don't want Sidney."

"Listen, you. I want someone strong here. Someone who's used to taking care of himself. Sidney can do that."

"I don't want Sidney."

"He's a responsible young boy, from what I hear, when he's not fighting with someone."

"I don't want Sidney. I want Charlie."

"Well, you're not having Charlie."

"But that's who I want."

"Well, forget it."

"Why?"

"Because I said so."

"No."

"I beg your pardon?"

"No."

"No what?"

"No, I won't forget it."

"Yes, you will."

"I want Charlie."

Elizabeth closed her eyes and rubbed her forehead. Already, she was feeling tired and overwhelmed and her mother wasn't even in the hospital yet. She was upstairs in her bedroom, thumping her foot on the floor for clean laundry to put into her suitcase.

"I know," said Jeffrey, after a moment. "How about both?"

Elizabeth opened her eyes and felt sick to her stomach.

"Why not?" said Jeffrey. "We'll keep him company while Grandma's having her operation. We'll keep his mind off things. We won't do anything bad. Charlie's parents live right here in town. Sidney's mom lives just over there. You can call them if something happens."

Elizabeth had to think. But really, when she thought about it, she didn't have to. Her son, a loner for the first twelve years of his life, was, in his own way, and likely without even realizing it, planning the first sleepover he'd ever had. So what if it was with a couple of kids who were not cut from the mould of perfection? Who was?

"All right," she said, quietly, reaching for her teacup. "Okay. Have them both."

Jeffrey clenched his fist and threw a punch into the air. "Yes," he said.

2

Elizabeth could not recall seeing him so happy.

Charlie arrived first, right after school, just as Jeffrey's mother had asked him not to do.

"Hello," he called out, sticking his round, fat face through the front door of the house. "Anybody home?"

Charlie was a chubby boy who talked endlessly and ate just as often. He lived with his mother, Bella, his dad, Ray, and his four older sisters.

He brought to Jeffrey's house a full-size suitcase, an overnight bag slung over his shoulder, two smaller bags by his feet, and two more bags behind him at the bottom of the front steps.

"Hello," he called out again when no one answered.

Then he heard footsteps.

"What are you doing here?" said Jeffrey, running quickly to the door, his eyes wide with panic. The reason Jeffrey's mother had asked the boys not to arrive early was a simple one: she wanted to get Grandma out the door with as little fuss as possible, meaning no visitors, and certainly no houseguests. Once Grandma was away, Charlie and Sidney could slip into the basement while Grandpa was having one of his daily naps. That way, there would be no balking at the arrangement, and no chance (or reason) for Grandma to reverse her decision to have the surgery and stay home.

"What am I doing here?" said Charlie. "What do you think I'm doing here?"

Jeffrey's face turned pink. "I told you not to come before six."

Charlie shrugged his shoulders. "My sister went out early. It was my last chance for a ride."

Jeffrey closed his eyes to think. This was exactly what his mother had told him to prevent.

"You know, she charged me two bucks for gas for driving from my house to here," said Charlie, unaware of the stress he was causing. "That's like four blocks. Two bucks for four blocks. And she wouldn't open the trunk until I paid her." He shook his head. "She's like a cab driver. A natural-born cab driver. How's that for a compliment?"

"Okay, Charlie," said Jeffrey, a new version of the plan in his head. "Pick up your bags and follow me."

"Maybe I should rob her the next time she gives me a ride."

"Charlie. Pick up your bags and follow me."

"Hey," said Charlie, who was not sharing in Jeffrey's rush to get moving. "What am I, the only guy in this town with arms? First her, now you. Charlie, get your bags. Charlie, pick up your stuff. Charlie, get your junk out of the trunk of my car. Charlie, grab everything and follow me."

Jeffrey moved back to the front door and grabbed the biggest suitcase. "Ouch," he said, straining his back. "What do you have in here?"

Charlie smiled. "Videos," he said, lifting his eyebrows. "Triple X. And magazines that'll make your head spin."

Jeffrey dropped the suitcase. "What?"

"Hey," said Charlie. "Be careful with that. My dad will kill me if anything happens to the stuff in there."

Jeffrey stood straight and looked at his friend. "Tell me you're joking."

"About what?"

"About what you just said."

"What did I just say?"

"About the contents of this suitcase."

Charlie glanced down at the suitcase, then up again. His face was pure innocence. "Why would I be joking about the contents of the suitcase?"

Jeffrey took in a deep breath and let his shoulders sag. "You are not bringing x-rated videos into this house, Charlie."

"Why not?"

"Because. It's not that kind of house."

"It's not what kind of house?"

"That kind of house. My grandparents live here, for Pete's sake. And before that, their parents lived here."

"So?"

"So my mother's a librarian."

"So what?"

"She doesn't watch this kind of stuff."

"Sure she does."

"She'd have a heart attack."

"She'd be smiling."

"She would not."

"Of course she would. Besides, who says we have to watch them with the whole family? This isn't Walt Disney. We put these on when the old guy's taking a nap. Your grandma's gonna be two hundred miles away."

"It doesn't matter, Charlie."

"Sure it does."

"Not in this house."

"Oh, come on."

"No."

"How about this."

"Forget it."

"I'll put one on, and we'll vote on it. You, Sidney and me. Majority rules."

"Sidney?" said Jeffrey.

Charlie nodded. "He gets the third vote."

"Sidney's probably seen all these movies ten times."

Charlie gave Jeffrey a look. "These are classics, my friend. No kid under twenty has seen these ten times."

Jeffrey shook his head and looked at the ceiling for help. Then, in an unexpected form, he got it.

Grandma Anderson, wrapped in her winter coat, boots, hat and scarf, walked slowly through the living room and stopped near the two boys at the front door.

At eighty-five years old, and in immediate need of heart surgery, she was not in her finest form, but her fiery eyes could still slice a diamond in two, and her bony fingers could make a young boy wince if she grabbed him by the shoulder.

"Jeffrey," she said, her voice strong, but tired.

"Yes, Grandma," said Jeffrey, turning to face her.

"I thought you were bringing my bags to the car."

Jeffrey gulped.

"And who are you talking to?"

"Um."

Charlie stepped forward. "Hello, Mrs. Anderson," he said, extending his hand. "I'm sorry to hear you're not feeling well."

Grandma Anderson looked at Charlie, then back at her grandson. "This boy looks familiar," she said.

Jeffrey gulped again and licked his lips.

"You look familiar, too," said Charlie, turning on the charm. "You're the young lady who used to work at the hardware store here in town."

Grandma Anderson leveled her eyes at

Charlie. At any age, she was not a woman to be toyed with or talked to like a Barbie doll.

"When are you leaving?" she said.

"Five days," said Charlie, with a smile.

"Five what?"

"Five days, counting today, which is really only a half, I know. But if we stay up 'til midnight, that's almost eight hours."

Standing slightly behind his grandma, Jeffrey closed his eyes and very slowly started to shake his head. Then, from the kitchen, he heard the unmistakable sound of his grandfather carrying something heavy. He turned to watch. Grandpa Anderson was a tall rail of a man with tufts of white hair clinging to his head and stubble on his face that rubbed against skin like coarse sandpaper. He was eighty-eight years old. He was half-dragging, half-carrying a suitcase.

Jeffrey moved to help him.

"Forget it," said Grandpa Anderson, waving him off. He came to a stop at the door.

"This young man says he's spending five days at the house while I'm gone," said Grandma, pointing to Charlie.

Grandpa Anderson, out of breath and making sure the suitcase didn't fall over, didn't hear her.

"Did you hear me?" said Grandma.

"What?" said Grandpa, adjusting his hearing aid.

"I said, 'This young man says he's staying here for five days while I'm gone.'"

Grandpa looked at her. "Are you saying something?"

"Yes, I'm saying something," said Grandma.

"I think I turned this thing off instead of on," he said, fiddling with his ear.

"Oh, for God's sake," said Grandma, her lips starting to tighten.

"I need a new plug," said Grandpa.

"You need more than that."

Grandpa pulled the hearing aid out of his ear and looked at it. "I'll call the doctor in the morning."

"You won't call anyone in the morning. You won't be able to hear what they're saying to you. You get Jeffrey to call in the morning."

"Crazy thing," said Grandpa, putting it back in his ear.

"That's why Charlie's staying over, Grandma," said Jeffrey. "He's going to help me with Grandpa."

Grandma Anderson looked again at

Charlie. Her face was as stern as a teacher's in the detention hall. Then she looked at Grandpa, and Jeffrey saw in her eyes that she knew she had no choice. Where once they had stood like pillars, withstanding all that nature and mankind could throw at them, his grandparents now needed help making phone calls and getting out the door, and that was really just the beginning.

She looked at Jeffrey and said nothing.

Jeffrey's mother arrived a moment later and the procession out the door began. Charlie moved his bags off the steps and into the house. Elizabeth gave him a piercing look before smiling politely and saying hello. She told Jeffrey they would call as soon as they arrived at the hospital. Jeffrey gave his grandma a hug and a kiss on the cheek and wished her good luck and told her he would see her soon. She looked up the front steps at Grandpa, who had stayed in the house, and waved goodbye. He waved back, then he came outside and carefully down the stairs and kissed her.

Jeffrey had never seen his grandparents kiss before.

He looked over at Charlie and Charlie gave him a wink and said, under his breath, "I bet they've seen a few movies in their day."

Jeffrey shook his head and returned to worrying about Charlie and the contents of his stupid suitcase.

3

Sidney arrived just after 7:00. He was out of breath, and the knuckles on his right hand were bleeding.

He carried a small bag under his arm.

Charlie and Jeffrey greeted him at the door.

"What's the matter with you?" said Jeffrey, who was already having second thoughts about the people he had invited to his house.

Sidney hesitated before answering.

He was not a big boy, but he was lean and quick and he fought as often as Charlie told a story.

"I just got in a fight," he said, his chest heaving slightly.

"You what?" said Jeffrey.

"Wow," said Charlie, moving closer to the door.

"I tuned him in," said Sidney. He tossed Charlie his bag and stepped inside the house.

Charlie looked at the bag, which was small and light and felt only half-full, and said, "What's this?"

"It's my stuff," said Sidney.

"Your stuff for what?"

"What do you think, my stuff for what? My stuff for staying here."

Charlie looked at the bag again. His own belongings were still in a heap in Jeffrey's basement. "This is it?"

"Yes."

Charlie gave the bag a little shake.

"There's nothing in here."

"Sure there is."

"Not very much."

"I brought everything I need."

Charlie shook the bag one more time. "Don't you wear underwear?"

"What?" said Sidney.

"There's nothing in here. It feels like all you've got is a toothbrush and a pair of socks."

Sidney moved forward and snapped the bag out of Charlie's hands. "I said, I've got everything I need. And of course I wear under-wear."

"Who did you get in a fight with?" said Jeffrey.

Sidney glared at Charlie for a moment, then moved back towards the door. "This guy," he said.

"What guy?" said Jeffrey.

"I just told you."

"No, you didn't."

"I said it was this guy," said Sidney. "This guy who gave my mom a hard time at the restaurant. He followed her home, so I tuned him in."

"How?" said Jeffrey.

"By laying him out on the street outside our apartment, that's how. He drove up to our entrance and I popped him one."

"He drove up?" said Charlie.

"Yes."

"In a car?"

"No. In a truck."

"So, he's like, sixteen?"

"No."

"Seventeen?"

"No."

"How old is he?"

"He's twenty-five," said Sidney.

Charlie's jaw dropped. Jeffrey's face turned as pink as fresh-cut grapefruit.

"Twenty-five?" said Charlie.

"That's what my mom said."

"You just punched a twenty-five year old?"

"Yes."

"In the face?"

"Yes."

"And now you're standing here out of breath because you ran here after punching him and you didn't want him to follow you?"

Sidney shrugged his shoulders. "Sort of."

"Sort of?" said Charlie.

"All right. Yes."

"And were you successful?" said Charlie.

"In what?"

"In getting here without him following you?"

"No."

Charlie's jaw dropped again, and Jeffrey, who looked like he might never talk again, sat down on the staircase.

"You weren't?" said Charlie.

Sidney shook his head. "No. They followed me. I saw their truck."

"*They* followed you?" said Charlie.

"There were two of them."

"How old was the other guy, forty?"

"He was about the same age," said Sidney. "I ran into the backyard and they drove by the house. I don't think they know for sure if I went into this place or not."

Charlie thought for a moment. "So they know which block you're on, and which side of the street, but not exactly which house."

Sidney nodded. "That's right."

"But they can probably figure out which house because they know where you disappeared off the street."

Sidney shrugged. "Maybe. Maybe not."

"Or they could cook up some story and go door-to-door looking for you."

"Possibly."

"Or they could just sit out there in their nice warm car and wait for you to step outside."

Sidney nodded. He was the only one of the three who did not look concerned. "Yes. They could probably do that."

"Well, that's terrific," said Charlie, looking briefly at Jeffrey.

"Hey, I did it for my mom," said Sidney.

"That's really good."

"If you don't like it, you can leave."

"Not really," said Charlie.

"Why not?"

"What if they see me? A twelve-year-old boy walking out of a house? They'd come after me for sure."

"So what? Tell them I'm here."

"Yeah," said Charlie. "I'll tell them you're here. And then we can have a big fight in Jeffrey's living room."

"I'll take them on outside," said Sidney.

"I should invite them in for a video, that's what I should do," said Charlie.

Jeffrey closed his eyes and took a deeper-than-usual breath.

"What video?" said Sidney.

"Never mind," said Jeffrey, with as much authority as he could find.

"What video?" said Sidney, looking at Charlie.

"Never mind," said Charlie, who actually did not feel like watching a video at the moment.

"I could go for a video," said Sidney, to no one in particular.

Then he walked into the living room of Jeffrey's grandparents' home and made himself comfortable, as if nothing at all had just happened and the next five days of his life were going to be full of fun and nothing else. "I think a video's a good idea," he said, putting his feet up.

Certainly better than punching a twenty-five year old in the face, thought Charlie to himself, but he didn't bother to say it out loud. Apparently, there was enough to deal with already.

In spite of his age and his own failing health and the fact that he had barely eaten a bite of food or closed his eyes for a moment of restful sleep since learning that Grandma needed surgery, Grandpa Anderson was still reasonably quick at figuring things out.

So it did not take him long to determine that Charlie was the big-mouth son of that obnoxious woman who had a head like a buffalo and the voice of a dragon who used to come into his hardware store. "Where's the deals?" she used to say, marching down the aisles like she owned the place. "It's cheaper in the city, y'know," she would add at the till.

He also knew darn well that Sidney was the prize son of Tizzy Martin, a middle-aged floozy who ran around today like she had twenty years ago, when he used to watch her through the window of his store.

The woman was a looker, there was no questioning that, but trouble followed her around like an obedient dog, and there had been several times in the past when Anderson's Hardware Supplies Shop had served as her own personal fire hydrant.

So it was with no small effort on his part that he set about keeping his tongue in check when Jeffrey brought his friends into the kitchen for a formal round of introductions. Grandpa was sitting at the table with a late supper of cold mashed potatoes in front of him. He had decided not to heat them, partly because then he would have to throw out what he didn't finish, according to Grandma's rules, but mainly because he could not recall exactly how the microwave worked.

"Grandpa?" Jeffrey had said, poking his head into the room.

"Right here," said Grandpa, hearing the boy clearly. He had fixed his hearing aid shortly after Grandma and Elizabeth had left.

"Grandpa," said Jeffrey again. He cleared his throat. "These are my two friends, Grandpa.

They're going to be staying over for the next couple of days, just to help out around the house and everything."

Grandpa eyed the two boys without speaking.

"This one's Sidney," said Jeffrey. Sidney gave the old man a quick wave and a nod of his head. "And this is Charlie."

Charlie stepped forward and saluted. "At your service, sir."

Grandpa Anderson said nothing.

Charlie stepped back in line with Jeffrey and Sidney.

"So," said Jeffrey, growing more nervous by the second, " we're just gonna do our thing and go to school and everything, and if you need our help for anything, just ask. Okay?"

Grandpa continued to look in silence at the three boys.

"Okay?" said Jeffrey again. "Okay. Well, anyway, I just wanted to introduce you to everybody and everything but now we'll go back downstairs. We'll go back to doing what we were doing. But this one's Sidney and this one's Charlie, in case you get them mixed up."

"I'm the good-looking one," said Charlie, throwing the old man a wink. "But he's the one with the girlfriend, so go figure."

Jeffrey felt a now-familiar twinge of fear as Charlie started to talk.

"There are no girls here, though, Grandpa," he said, very quickly. "There's not going to be anything like that. We're just here to hold the fort while Grandma and Mom are gone."

"Hey," said Charlie, "that's not what you told me."

Jeffrey's heart began to thump. "What?"

"You said the show starts nightly at 10:00."

"I what?"

"You said the show starts nightly at 10:00."

"I did not."

"Isn't that what he said to you?" said Charlie, turning to Sidney.

"Shut up," said Sidney.

"Didn't he say that to you? I can't remember now if he said nine or ten."

"There are no girls here, Charlie," said Jeffrey forcefully.

Charlie checked his watch. "I know. They're late. What's taking them so long?"

Jeffrey's eyes started to burn like cinders.

"Last week at the Boy Scout camp they were on time every night."

"Knock it off, Charlie," said Sidney, stepping forward.

Jeffrey turned to his grandpa who was still slowly working his way through his first bite of potatoes and staring at the boys. "There are no girls here, Grandpa. Charlie's only joking around."

"Tell Grandpa you're joking around, Charlie," said Sidney.

"All right. You're joking around, Charlie," said Charlie.

Sidney took another step and then used a move that the boys had not learned at karate: he put Charlie in a headlock.

"Hey!" said Charlie, starting to flail.

"Tell Grandpa you're joking, Charlie," said Sidney.

"Guys, please don't fight," said Jeffrey.

"Tell Grandpa you're joking, Charlie," said Sidney again, through clenched teeth.

"All right. Okay," said Charlie. Sidney released his grip.

"Tell him," he said.

"All right," said Charlie, twisting his head from side-to-side. Then he turned to face Grandpa Anderson.

"I was only joking about the shows," he

said. "They're not going to happen."

At any other time in his life, having seen a display like this, Grandpa Anderson likely would have reached out and grabbed a fistful of fat on Charlie's arm or belly or neck and squeezed it until the boy stopped talking. But this time, he did nothing. He was too overwhelmed by his thoughts. For years he had felt in touch with young people. Now, sitting there in his own kitchen, an unbearable sense of loneliness descending upon his shoulders, he felt like a man in a foreign country, unable to communicate with the local population and, for all intents and purposes, excluded from their plans.

"I do have some videos that'll set your clock back a few years," said Charlie, before anyone could stop him. "Feel free to join us if you'd like to do that."

"Don't mind if I do," Grandpa said. He surprised even himself when he said it. Collectively, the three boys reacted as if they'd been jolted with a cattle prod.

"You what?" said Charlie.

Grandpa licked the dryness from his lips and set his spoon down beside his potatoes. Not even during the war did he miss his wife

Edna as much as he did now. "If you have some videos, I'd be glad to watch them."

Jeffrey immediately stepped forward. "Charlie was only joking, Grandpa," he said.

"Didn't sound like it to me," said the old man.

"Well—" said Jeffrey.

"I was," said Charlie. "Sort of."

"You either were or you weren't," said Grandpa Anderson. "Make up your mind."

Just talking was making him feel better.

"Well, I was," said Charlie. "Sort of."

"Charlie," said Jeffrey.

"Make up your mind, boy," said Grandpa.

"I'm trying to," said Charlie.

"Charlie!" said Jeffrey.

"I'm trying to," said Charlie.

"What's so wrong with your grandpa watching videos with us?" said Sidney.

Jeffrey turned and stared in confounded amazement at Sidney. Then he realized that Charlie had talked about the videos before Sidney had arrived at the house.

"It's not a good idea," said Jeffrey, keeping it simple.

"Why not?"

"Because it's not a good idea," said Jeffrey

again, staring hard into Sidney's eyes in the hopes of conveying the message not to push it.

"You've said that twice," said Sidney. "I still want to know why."

"Trust me," said Jeffrey, widening his eyes.

"Why should I trust you?" said Sidney. "And why are you looking at me like some sort of freak?"

Jeffrey dropped the stare and went back to work on Charlie. "Charlie, tell Grandpa that you were joking, all right? Tell him you were kidding around."

Charlie thought for a moment, then he motioned for Jeffrey to come closer.

"Don't you see how lonely he looks?" he said, dropping his voice to just above a whisper.

"So what?" said Jeffrey, hissing like a cat.

"So let's see what we can do for him."

"Charlie, are you nuts? You've got X-rated videos downstairs in your suitcase. I can't let Grandpa see those."

"Might make him feel better," said Charlie.

"Charlie! My mom will kill me. She'll kill you, too. Now drop it. We'll take him out for an ice cream or something. Or a hamburger."

Charlie considered that for a moment. "We could have ice cream and watch the videos at the same time," he said.

Jeffrey started to burn. For the first time in his life, he turned deep red for a reason that had nothing to do with intense fear. He was about to speak, but Sidney cut him off.

"What are you guys doing?" he said, stepping into the huddle.

"Movie talk," said Charlie.

"Charlie wants to show my grandpa the X-rated films he swiped from his dad's closet," said Jeffrey.

"Hey, I didn't swipe them," said Charlie.

"You've got X-rated films?" said Sidney.

Charlie gave him a sly wink. "Four-star rating," he said.

"What are we doing here then?" said Sidney.

"Exactly," said Jeffrey, desperate to get out of the kitchen. "Tell my grandpa you were joking around and let's go downstairs."

"Is this what you were talking about back there?" said Sidney.

"Yes," said Jeffrey.

"But he looks so lonely over there," said

Charlie. "God, he's sitting here in his very own kitchen eating a bowl of cold mashed potatoes by himself. His wife of ninety years is getting split open in the morning. His daughter left him to be with her. And now his only grandson wants to ditch him to watch dirty videos in the basement."

Jeffrey stared at Charlie. "This is all your idea, Charlie. I didn't ask you to bring those things over here."

"That is pretty lousy, you know," said Sidney, turning to Jeffrey.

"Of course it is," said Charlie.

"I mean, the least you could do is get the guy some hot food," said Sidney.

"Get the guy some meat," said Charlie. "He's got real teeth, doesn't he? He can eat meat."

Jeffrey closed his eyes and took in a deep breath.

"I mean, I don't know whose idea it was or what, but I gotta go with Charlie on this one," said Sidney.

"It was Charlie's idea," said Jeffrey, his eyes still closed.

"You can't just leave the old guy up here starving while you run downstairs and turn the TV on," said Sidney.

"I wasn't even thinking about it until Jeffrey mentioned something about girls," said Charlie.

Jeffrey started to rub his forehead.

"I think we should make the old guy some eggs," said Sidney.

"That's a terrific idea," said Charlie, nodding his head.

"I'll make him an omelet," said Sidney.

"I'll slice the ham," said Charlie.

"We don't need ham," said Sidney.

"We don't have any ham," said Jeffrey, who now just wanted to go upstairs to his room and curl up and go to bed.

"Well, I'll get the sausages then. Or the bacon," said Charlie.

"We don't need sausages," said Sidney. "And we don't need bacon."

"Well, what kind of an omelet is that?" said Charlie. "No bacon. No ham. No sausages."

"It's a cheese omelet," said Sidney.

"Just cheese?"

"And a little pepper. It's my specialty. I make my mom one practically every night."

"That sounds as boring as a cheese pizza," said Charlie.

"That's my favorite kind," said Sidney.

"You're kidding."

"No. Why would I kid about that?"

Charlie shrugged his shoulders. "No reason."

"Yes, there is. Now what is it? Why would I kid about that?"

"Well, come on," said Charlie. "I mean, you got this big, flat, smooth surface just sitting there waiting for you to put something on it, and all you can come up with is a few little bits of white cheese?"

"Well, what do you put on your pizza? Hot dogs? Onion rings?"

"I've had a hot dog pizza before," said Charlie. "It tasted just fine."

"Guys," said Jeffrey.

"I bet you have," said Sidney.

"I know I have," said Charlie.

"I bet you probably wrapped the whole thing in a gigantic bun too, didn't you," said Sidney.

"Guys," said Jeffrey.

"No. And I didn't smear it with ketchup or mustard, either. But it was still a good pizza."

"I bet it was disgusting," said Sidney.

"Well at least it wasn't some plain Jane

hunk of dough with sauce and cheese on it," said Charlie.

"Guys. Knock it off. My grandpa's sitting there waiting for us to say something to him," said Jeffrey.

"Ask him what he wants on his pizza," said Charlie.

"I'm not making pizza," said Sidney.

"On his omelet then," said Charlie.

"You ask him," said Jeffrey.

"You ask him," said Charlie. "He's your relative."

"You ask him," said Jeffrey.

"Excuse me, Mr. Anderson," said Sidney, turning away from the others. "Would you mind if I made you something hot to eat?"

"What's that?" said Grandpa, who had almost started to doze as the boys held their discussion.

"I'd like to make you an omelet. I make my mom one every night and I was wondering if I could make you one tonight."

Grandpa thought for a moment. "What do you put in it?" he said.

"Cheese," said Charlie, cutting in. "We're talking about a plain old cheese omelet here."

"Is that it?" said the old man.

"That's it," said Sidney, glaring at Charlie.

"And some pepper," said Charlie. "For flavor."

"Well, that sounds pretty good to me," said Grandpa Anderson. "I can't have much more than that at this time of night anyway. Gives me gas."

The three boys looked at each other. For a moment, they weren't quite sure what to do, then Sidney broke away and opened the fridge to get the eggs out. Charlie sidled over to the table and sat down. And Jeffrey, wishing he could wind the clock back so he could change a few of the decisions he had made, stood still and watched his friends take care of his grandfather.

At 7:00 the following night the doorbell rang. The three boys, sitting downstairs debating what to watch on television, froze.

Jeffrey ran to a window and looked to see who it was, but all he could make out was a pair of feet standing on the top step at the front door.

"Who is it?" said Charlie.

"I can't see anything," said Jeffrey. "All I can see is a pair of feet."

"How many?" said Sidney.

Jeffrey turned and looked at him. "How many what?"

"How many feet?"

"I just said I see a pair."

"Do you see one foot or two?" said Sidney.

Jeffrey frowned for a moment and then turned to take a second look. "I see two. Two black-booted feet. Both the same."

Sidney started to relax. "It's not him then," he said.

"It's not the guy you punched?" said Charlie.

"No."

"How do you know?" said Jeffrey.

"You would have only seen one foot."

Charlie and Jeffrey exchanged glances.

"You mean you punched a one-legged man in the face?" said Charlie.

Sidney gave him a look. "He happened to be on crutches, okay?"

"On crutches?" said Jeffrey.

"That's what I said."

"So you did punch a one-legged man in the face," said Charlie.

"He wasn't a one-legged man. He has two perfectly fine legs but one of them happens to be in a cast at the moment."

"Well, that pretty well makes him one-legged," said Charlie.

"No, it doesn't."

"Sure it does."

"No, it doesn't."

"Of course it does."

"It does not."

"Look. Just because the guy's not an amputee doesn't mean he's not one-legged. You said yourself he's got crutches."

"So?"

"So he's got crutches because he's only got one leg. He's got one working leg. That's where the crutches come in."

"Well, so what?" said Sidney, getting angry. "What if he didn't have any legs? What difference would it make?"

"Apparently it wouldn't make any difference at all to you," said Charlie. "You'd just bend down and smack him anyway."

The doorbell rang again. Jeffrey watched as the two feet at the top of the steps started to stamp lightly in the snow. "I think it's a woman," he said.

"Is she in heels?" said Charlie.

"No," said Jeffrey.

"Why would a woman be going door-to-door in winter in high heels?" said Sidney.

"I don't know," said Charlie. "Maybe if her car broke down."

"I think it's my Auntie Ivy," said Jeffrey.

The boys heard a pounding on the door.

"And I don't think she's going away until someone lets her in."

Jeffrey ran upstairs and opened the front door and let his Auntie Ivy into the house.

She was a short, almost perfectly round woman with a pleasant-enough face and a chattering disposition. She was Jeffrey's grandma's youngest sister.

"Jeffrey," she said, her face aglow. She cupped her hands around his cheeks. "How's my little man doing? How's my boy?"

"I'm fine thanks, Auntie," said Jeffrey, stepping back.

Auntie Ivy removed her mittens and the scarf she had wrapped around her head as a shawl and handed them to Jeffrey. She then began to unbutton her coat.

"Brrr," she said. "It's a cold one out there tonight."

She handed her coat to Jeffrey and bent down to take off her boots.

Jeffrey stood still. He was unsure what to do. He had not been told by his mom that Auntie Ivy would be coming by the house, and he was certain that she had not been invited by Grandpa, since Grandpa did not like his sister-in-law Ivy very much. He did not enjoy the company of his sisters-in-law Rose and Beatrice, either, but as far as Jeffrey could recall, Auntie Ivy was the one he talked about the most.

"You just put all that away in the closet for me, dear. I'll pass you these boots as soon as I get them off."

Jeffrey remained still, not out of defiance, but because he was trying to figure out what was going on.

His aunt straightened up and handed him her boots. "Is there a problem?" she said when she saw that he hadn't moved.

"Um," said Jeffrey.

His aunt smiled, then raised her eyebrows. She was waiting for an answer.

"It's just."

"Just what, dear?"

"I'm just, I'm just wondering what you're doing here."

Auntie Ivy's eyebrows dropped like bricks as she frowned.

"Is my sister not in the hospital?" she said.

"Yes."

"And did my niece Elizabeth not go with her?"

"Yes. She did."

"So does that not put you here alone with your grumpy old grandfather?"

"No."

"It doesn't?"

"No. I'm here with some friends. I have some friends helping me."

"Oh, you do?"

"Yes."

"So that's how your mother chose to arrange it. Rather than calling upon family in a time of need, she got her twelve-year-old son to invite some of his friends over to the house."

"That's not exactly right, Auntie," said Jeffrey, soft shades of pink appearing on his face.

"Oh, I'm sure it's not, dear. But we don't have to quibble over details. The long and the short of it is, my very own sister is having major heart surgery, and I found out about it from one of your neighbors who saw her leaving the house with a suitcase."

Jeffrey said nothing.

"But never mind. We're not here for long. We won't spoil your fun for more than a night."

"We?" said Jeffrey.

"Your Uncle Unger is parking the car."

Jeffrey briefly closed his eyes and reminded himself to stay calm.

"And he's not in a very good mood," said Auntie Ivy, already busying herself in the living room. The day's newspaper had been left untouched on the floor. She picked it up and put it neatly on the coffee table. She took an empty drinking glass from one of the shelves and very quickly, instinctively almost, ran a finger across the wood to check for dust. "You know your uncle. Nothing seems to ever bother him, but when something does bother him, it really bothers him."

Out of respect, Jeffrey nodded in agreement with his aunt, but the truth of the matter was, Uncle Unger had not enjoyed a happy moment in his entire life.

So went the stories, anyway.

"So, anyway," said Auntie Ivy, heading towards the kitchen, "please be on your best behavior. And you might want to pass on a cautionary word to your friends, too, wherever they are."

Jeffrey sucked in a deep breath as he remembered that Charlie and Sidney were downstairs. Then, as if summoned by his thoughts, Charlie called out from the bottom of the staircase, "Hey, Jeffrey. The movie's on."

Jeffrey froze for a moment, the full impact of Charlie's words taking a second to kick in. Then he bolted past his aunt like an Olympic sprinter and took the stairs three-at-a-time. He came to a screeching stop in front of the television. His eyes wide with panic, he checked the screen. The movie the boys had put on was *Shrek*, an animated film about a monster.

"What's this?" Jeffrey said, catching his breath.

"It's *Shrek*," said Charlie. "It's hilarious."

"I haven't seen it," said Sidney. "Get out of the way so I can see the screen."

"I thought you guys were watching something else," said Jeffrey.

"Like what?" said Sidney.

"Like one of those videos Charlie brought from his dad's closet."

Sidney raised an eyebrow and looked at Jeffrey. "You think we were gonna put one of those on when you're having a family reunion upstairs?"

"You can't get those things out of your mind, can you?" said Charlie.

Jeffrey's heart rate remained high. He was in distress, and the relief at not seeing on the television what he thought he was going to see was quickly replaced by thoughts of what was going to happen when his grandfather returned home from his regular trip to the Legion.

"Last night you were talking about them. Today at school you were talking about them."

"I asked you to get them out of here," said Jeffrey. "I'm the one who wants nothing to do with those stupid things."

Charlie nodded. "Sure you are."

"I am."

"Hey," said Sidney, shifting in his seat so he could see the TV. "You guys mind?"

Jeffrey took two steps to the right and nearly collided with his Auntie Ivy, who had just arrived in the basement.

"Hello, again," she said, her face a ball of good cheer; her eyes darting around the room like cat burglars in a jewelry store. "These must be the boys you were telling me about."

Sidney immediately straightened himself in his chair, and Charlie leapt to his feet like a new player in a game show.

"Yes. Yes, they are," said Jeffrey.

"Hello, boys. I'm Jeffrey's Auntie Ivy."

"Hello," said Charlie.

"Hi," said Sidney.

"Enjoying the movie?"

"Sure are," said Charlie.

"Hasn't started yet," said Sidney.

Charlie turned and gave Sidney a look.

"It's the previews," said Sidney.

Auntie Ivy turned to Jeffrey. "Now what was this about movies from Charlie's closet?" she said. "I heard you discussing them as I came down the stairs."

Jeffrey opened his mouth as if to speak, but no sounds were heard. Charlie moved closer and said, "Actually, we weren't talking about movies in Charlie's closet. It was a movie called 'In Charlie's Closet.' It's kind of a 'coming-out' story that I've been working on in my film class."

Auntie Ivy looked at Charlie but said nothing.

"It's pretty good, too," said Charlie, going on. "My teacher's going to send it to CBC when I'm done cutting it. He really likes it. It's a true story about my brother."

"Your brother?" she said.

"Yes."

"And it's a coming-out story?"

"Yes."

"Oh, my."

"Would that be your brother Guy?" said

Sidney, referring to a brother Charlie had invented once before.

"Uh, yes," said Charlie.

"The helicopter pilot?"

"You got it."

Auntie Ivy narrowed her eyes as she considered Charlie's story. She looked ready to launch into a more detailed line of questioning when she was interrupted by the front door opening and then closing upstairs.

"Oh, dear," she said, looking up. "That must be Unger. Jeffrey, come along and show me what food your mother has prepared. My guess is you'll be needing more already."

Jeffrey let out an invisible sigh of relief and went upstairs with his aunt. He said hello to his uncle. For the next few minutes, things went reasonably well, but then the front door opened again. This time, the long, lean, slightly shivering figure of Grandpa Anderson stepped into the house.

It took Grandpa a moment to notice that he had more visitors. When he did, he was not impressed. He stood silent for a moment, his coat on a hanger but not yet tucked away in the closet. "What brings you here, Unger?" he said.

"The wife," said Jeffrey's uncle. He was a short, stocky businessman who owned a chain of Laundromats. He unzipped his coat but kept it on. His feelings towards Grandpa Anderson were much the same as Grandpa Anderson's were to him.

"The what?" said Grandpa, turning to put his coat away.

"I said, 'The wife,'" said Uncle Unger. "She brought me here. She's concerned about her sister."

Grandpa finished with his coat and moved towards the kitchen.

"Well, if she's concerned about her sister, what the hell's she doing here?" He walked into the next room. Jeffrey was standing before the open fridge, pointing to the various foods and beverages on all the shelves, while Auntie Ivy looked on.

"I'll make you a soup," she said, when the boy finished.

"We're fine, Auntie," he said.

"Don't be silly. I'll cook you a roast and I'll make you some soup."

"Really. We don't need it," said Jeffrey.

"It's the least I can do for my poor sister," she said. "My poor sister whose husband didn't even call when she was taken to the hospital."

"I have all the next of kin I need right here," said Grandpa, motioning to Jeffrey.

"Oh, you," said Auntie Ivy.

"Oh, me is right," said Grandpa.

"Everything is always money, money, money with you, isn't it," said Auntie Ivy.

"Look in your own mirror before you start polishing mine," said Grandpa.

Auntie Ivy's nostrils started to flare. She turned to Jeffrey. "Did you know your grandpa sold us a drill one time for fifty dollars, even though the very same drill was on at Canadian Tire for twenty-five dollars, and he didn't even waive the tax on it? The darn thing broke as soon as we got it home."

"And he insisted there was no warranty," said Uncle Unger, joining in.

"Was this before or after the check bounced on that car you bought from me?" said Grandpa.

Auntie Ivy's eyes sprang wide open, and Uncle Unger's jaw clenched as tight as a bear trap.

"You know damn well that was a mistake," said Auntie Ivy.

"You bet it was," said Grandpa.

"You know what I mean."

"That's what I'm talking about."

"Ivy, get your coat," said Uncle Unger. "We're leaving."

He turned to leave the kitchen and nearly butted heads with Charlie who, along with Sidney, had slipped upstairs when the fighting broke out. "Who are you?" he said.

Charlie took a second to answer.

"Oh, this is Jeffrey's friend," said Auntie Ivy. "This is the help Elizabeth arranged for."

Uncle Unger glared at Charlie.

"Tell him about this movie of yours," said Auntie Ivy, leaving Jeffrey at the refrigerator.

"What movie?" said Uncle Unger.

Charlie said nothing.

"He's making a movie about his brother. A helicopter pilot who flew out of the closet."

Uncle Unger's glare grew hotter. "A what?" he said.

"He's making a movie about his brother who came out of the closet," said Auntie Ivy. "Tell him," she said to Charlie. "Go ahead. You were all chatty about it downstairs. You and your little friend there. Tell him. Go on. Tell him all about it."

Charlie gulped and cleared his throat. Sidney took a tiny, yet significant, step backwards down the hallway.

"I'm, I'm making a movie about my brother," said Charlie.

In the kitchen, Jeffrey started to say a silent prayer for absolutely anything to happen that would get him out of this.

"And he's a what?" said Uncle Unger.

"He's a pilot."

"I don't mean that. What else is he?"

"Uh. He's — ," said Charlie.

"He's too damn young to be making movies about that kind of thing, that's what he is," said Auntie Ivy. "It's ridiculous. And it's for school yet."

"It's what?" said Uncle Unger.

"His teacher likes it," said Auntie Ivy.

"Your teacher likes it?" said Uncle Unger.

"That's, that's what he said," said Charlie.

"And now you're hooked up with my nephew?" said Uncle Unger, taking a step forward.

"He has the movie downstairs," said Auntie Ivy. "I heard them talking about it."

"You have it downstairs?" said Uncle Unger.

Charlie gulped and said nothing.

"What are you bringing a movie like that to a house like this for?" said Uncle Unger.

"It's for school," said Charlie.

"Maybe we should go down and take a look at it then," said Uncle Unger. "See what all the excitement is about."

"Yes," said Auntie Ivy. "I think that's a good idea."

Sidney took another step down the hall, and Jeffrey, his legs like soggy tubes of cardboard, moved towards a chair to sit down.

"I'm not really finished it yet," said Charlie.

"You've finished enough to have a name for it," said Auntie Ivy.

"What's it called?" said Uncle Unger.

"'In Charlie's Closet' said Auntie Ivy.

"Good God," said Uncle Unger.

Auntie Ivy shook her head.

"Are you sure it's about your brother?" said Uncle Unger.

"Let's go downstairs and see what this is about," said Auntie Ivy, moving towards the door to the basement. "This is ridiculous."

"You stay out of my basement," said Grandpa Anderson, waving a once-strong finger in the air.

All talking stopped, and for some, all breathing.

"You stay out of my basement," he repeated.

Uncle Unger turned to face him. "You don't care what this boy's showing to your grandson?"

"I don't care for you to be in this house anymore. Now get out, and take her with you."

"Don't you refer to me as 'her,'" said Auntie Ivy.

"I'll refer to you any way I want," said Grandpa.

"Don't you refer to me as 'her.'"

"Come on, Ivy," said Uncle Unger. "I told you this was a mistake."

"You got that right," said Grandpa.

"Don't you ever refer to me as 'her' again," said Auntie Ivy.

"Oh, get out," said Grandpa.

A moment later, they were gone. And a moment after that, the three boys, so relieved they couldn't speak, were back in the basement.

To ease the tension created by the visit with Auntie Ivy and Uncle Unger, the boys dug into their homework. Jeffrey pulled out the Math he had to do, while Sidney and Charlie started writing paragraphs for Language Arts.

Sidney finished writing his first and sat back and read it out loud. When he was done, Charlie said, "Read that last bit again," and leaned forward in his chair, as if to listen even closer.

"Why?" said Sidney, who had not been looking for help.

"I'm not sure it makes any sense."

"I don't care if you think it makes any sense."

"Then why did you read it out loud?"

"Because I happen to like reading my work out loud. It makes it clearer in my head."

Charlie thought about that for a moment, then he nodded. "All right. Fair enough."

"So, I wasn't reading it to you, all right? I was reading it to me."

"Okay. How did it sound?"

"It sounded fine."

"All right then," said Charlie. "Forget about it."

Sidney looked at his paper. "It sounded just the way I wanted it to sound."

"Even the last part?" said Charlie.

"Yes."

Charlie made a face, as if to say that he was surprised to hear that, and left it alone.

Sidney read his paragraph over again, this time to himself. He picked up his pen and made a few changes, then he read it again.

"So why aren't you reading it out loud now?" said Charlie.

"I don't feel like it."

"I thought you just said it makes it clearer in your head."

"Sometimes it does, sometimes it doesn't," said Sidney. He made another change to his paragraph.

"Did you change that last part yet?" said Charlie.

"No. What last part?"

"The part at the end."

Sidney read over the last few lines of his paragraph. He made a small change and put down his pen.

"What did you change?" said Charlie.

"I changed the last part."

"What part of it?"

Sidney read it one more time to himself and made another change to the last line.

"What part of it?" said Charlie again.

Sidney told him specifically which part he had changed.

"Why'd you change that?"

Sidney looked at Charlie, then back at his paper.

"I liked that part," said Charlie. "That was the only part of the last part that I liked."

Sidney gave his work another careful read. The assignment was Write About Your Home, and he had chosen to detail every square foot of it, beginning with the hallway that led from the door of the little apartment he lived in with his mom, to the kitchen (on the left) and the living room (straight ahead).

The start of his paragraph went like this: "When you walk through the door of my home you step into a small hallway. There is a picture of me as a baby on one side of it, and a picture of my mom as a baby on the other. There are no pictures of my dad anywhere in the entire apartment, which, according to my mom, is no accident."

"See," said Charlie. "I liked the whole start of the thing, and the middle, but I don't like the end. The very last line. It doesn't work for me."

"What very last line?" said Sidney, as if there were several of them to choose from.

"That part where you say you wished you lived in a bigger home."

"What's wrong with that?"

"It doesn't fit."

"What do you mean it doesn't fit?"

"It doesn't work."

"It does so work."

"No, it doesn't."

Sidney read his paragraph to himself one more time.

"It's too mushy," said Charlie.

"It's too what?"

"I think you should read it out loud again."

Sidney put down his paper. "Didn't I tell

you that I didn't care what you thought?"

"Yes."

"So why are you still talking?"

"I can't help myself."

"You can so."

"I think you have the makings of a very good story there."

"So what?"

"But the ending doesn't work."

Sidney picked up his paper. Then he put it down again. "I told you I don't care. I like the ending just the way it is. Now butt out."

"But you've changed it once already."

"So what?"

"So maybe if you read it again, out loud, you'll change it again and make it right."

"It is right."

"That's what you said a few minutes ago."

"No. I told you to butt out a few minutes ago."

"No, you told me to butt out a few seconds ago."

"Well, I'm saying it again. Butt out. Mind your own business."

Charlie looked down at his own paper. "All right," he said, with a shrug. He started writing. Sidney stared at his own paper without reading it. He was angry. As a boy who actually enjoyed writing assignments like this one, he took careful pride in his work, and the marks he received often reflected his efforts. But this time, Charlie had messed him up.

"There is nothing wrong with this paper," he said, to no one in particular. "There is absolutely nothing wrong with it."

"If you say so," said Charlie.

"The ending is fine."

"Well, you can hand it in tomorrow with a smile on your face."

"And I've never written anything in my life that was too mushy."

"Maybe I used the wrong word then."

"Mushy is for people like you. You write the mushy stuff. I write stuff that's real."

"Maybe that's the problem," said Charlie, looking up from his paper.

"There is no problem."

"The last part isn't real."

"What?"

"The last part doesn't sound real. You write this whole piece about your apartment and all the things you and your mom have in it and how there's nothing in it about your dad, and at the end, all you say is you wished you lived in a bigger home."

"So?"

"So maybe that's not what you really wish," said Charlie.

Sidney said nothing for a moment. Sitting in the corner of the room at his desk, Jeffrey looked up briefly from his Math book.

"What?" said Sidney.

"I don't know," said Charlie, recognizing at once the change in feeling in the room. "Maybe that's not what you really wish for, that's all. Maybe you're really wishing for something else, but you just don't know it. Or maybe you do know it, but you don't want to write about it." He glanced briefly into Sidney's eyes and saw that he was suddenly not as tough as he said he was.

"Maybe it's not," said Sidney.

"So that's all I'm saying. Maybe you want to change it so it sounds as real as the rest of it."

Sidney read over his paper again, but he was not really reading it. His eyes just scanned the words on the page. "If you think I wanna see my dad again, you're wrong," he said after a moment, without looking up.

"I never said that," said Charlie.

"And if you think I wanna see a picture of him hanging in my room, you're wrong about that, too."

"I never said that either."

Sidney hesitated before speaking again. When he spoke he was still looking down at the table. "But you think the least the guy could do is ask for one of me."

The room went quiet.

"You know? Five years he's been gone and there hasn't been one phone call. Not one letter. It wasn't me who threw him out of the house. I had nothing to do with it. I was already in bed every night when they had their fights."

"Maybe he has one already," said Charlie, looking for the bright side.

Sidney shook his head. "Mom has all of them. In a box in her bedroom."

"That doesn't mean he doesn't still care about you," said Jeffrey, who knew what being left behind by your father was all about.

Sidney turned his head. "Oh, really?"

"Yes."

"And what therapist told you that? Dr. Morgan? Dr. Taylor? Dr. Armstrong?"

"Dr. Norton," said Jeffrey.

"Who's he?"

"It's a woman. She's in the city."

"Well, she uses the same stupid lines as these bozos out here do," said Sidney. "They must have all gone to college together. And the next time you see her, tell her they don't work."

Jeffrey looked back at his Math. He knew how useless lines like that could be, especially when you weren't feeling so good.

"Well, send him one anyway," said Charlie, returning to form. "Who cares if he didn't ask for it. Put one in an envelope and send it anyway. And if he returns it, send it back again."

Sidney stared at Charlie for a moment.

"Why not? Get a good picture of your-self and blow it up and send it to him."

Sidney thought about it. It wasn't a bad idea.

"Actually," said Charlie, "you know what you should do? Send him one of me, and put on it 'Love, Sidney,' so he thinks it's you he's looking at. That'll get him wondering where all the years have gone."

Sidney started to smile.

"I'll bet he'd stare at that picture for three

hours trying to figure out what happened."

"Or for two seconds before fainting," said Sidney, starting to laugh.

"I could pose with one of my sisters' friends at the outdoor pool this summer. You could write 'Aloha, from Hawaii!' on it. I could be holding one of those drinks with the little umbrellas in it. Have a big hat on. I'll wear my pink Speedo."

Sidney shook his head.

"You should do that," said Charlie.

Sidney looked back at his paragraph. It was a short laugh, but, as laughter often does, the air had been cleared, and he now saw what Charlie had been talking about.

He started to rewrite the ending.

"So, what are you putting down?" said Charlie.

Sidney didn't answer.

"Hey," said Charlie, anxious to hear the revision.

After a few minutes, Sidney put down his pen and read over to himself what he had written.

"Let's hear it," said Charlie.

Sidney read out loud the new ending.

"Beneath my mom's bed is a box of photographs of me that she protects like it's a live baby. Maybe one day I will take one of them out and send it to my dad, so he can put it on his wall and look at it. But for now, I won't bother. This is about my home. I don't even know what my dad's place looks like."

Charlie said, "See, that's what I was talking about," when Sidney finished reading. "That's real, from top to bottom."

Sidney nodded and read his work again.

Jeffrey, glad that he only had some simple Math problems to figure out, went back to his calculator.

The next morning, Sidney looked out the living-room window on his way to the breakfast table and saw the truck that had chased him to Jeffrey's house. It was an old, rusty, green-and-white pick-up, and it was moving very slowly down the street, as if the driver was looking for someone.

Sidney could not see if there was a passenger riding in the truck, but he imagined that there must have been.

He walked into the kitchen and didn't say a word. Charlie was sitting alone at the table, eating a bowl of Cheerios. Sidney stared absently at the table.

"You still feeling good about that paragraph you wrote?"

Sidney gave no indication that he had heard Charlie.

"I gotta finish mine after school."

Sidney sat down and tried to think. He did not feel like getting into anything today, especially a fight with a revenge-seeking twenty-five year old, whether he was on crutches or not.

"I thought we worked together pretty well last night," said Charlie. "I felt a bit of a bond going on there."

Sidney rose from the table and went and looked out the window again. He saw that the truck was making another pass down the street. Apparently, it was not going to leave until all the kids on the block had left for school.

He felt a familiar sense of anxiety begin to grow. The adrenaline that fueled the fury of his punches started to flow, and instinctively he began flexing his fingers into fists. Then Jeffrey walked into the living room. "Grandpa wants to go out with us today,"

"He what?" said Sidney, his pre-fight ritual interrupted.

"He wants to take us out and do something today."

"It's Wednesday," said Sidney.

"I know."

"So what's he talking about?"

Jeffrey shrugged. He had a small smile on his face. "He wants us to skip school and go do something."

"He what?" said Sidney again.

"He said he doesn't want to be alone today. He wants us to skip school and go do something. In the city."

Sidney could not believe what he was hearing. He moved closer to the living-room window. From an angle, he could see the pick-up waiting at the end of the street.

"What are you looking for?" said Jeffrey.

"Nothing," said Sidney.

Charlie walked into the room. A few drops of milk were trickling down his chin, but he was too excited to notice. "Did I just hear someone say that we've all been invited to skip school and spend a day in the city?"

"You sure did," said Jeffrey, starting to beam. This was entirely new territory for him, but, surprisingly, he was not concerned by what might happen if they were caught.

"You're serious?"

"I sure am."

"You're absolutely, positively serious?"

"You bet."

Charlie looked at Sidney and rubbed his

hands together. "Well, hey. I'd say this calls for a celebration."

"Like what?" said Jeffrey.

"Like I don't know. A few beer on the patio. A martini lunch. What do people do when they wake up in the morning thinking they have to do something and then find out they don't have to do it?"

"What time are we going?" said Sidney, looking out the window again.

"He said around 11:00," said Jeffrey.

"What are you looking at?" said Charlie.

"Nothing," said Sidney. He moved away from the window with a smile on his face. By 11:00, the pick-up truck would be long gone. "A celebration is a good idea. Let's go downstairs and think about it."

At 11:00 sharp, Sidney and Charlie sat in the living room with their coats on and their boots by the front door while Jeffrey ran upstairs. He walked downstairs a few minutes later and said that his grandpa was just waking up from a nap and would need another half-hour to get ready. Then he said, "He wants to take us to Tony's for lunch."

Charlie and Sidney exchanged glances.

"Tony's?" said Charlie, raising an eyebrow.

"Yes. For pizza."

"That's not exactly in the city," said Sidney.

Jeffrey shrugged. "It's his favorite place, other than the Legion. But he says there's no point going there if we can't drink beer."

"Who says we can't drink beer?" said Charlie, looking offended.

"He did."

"I can drink beer."

"No, you can't."

"Well, Sidney can drink beer."

"Not in a restaurant."

"You can drink beer."

"Not legally. And I've never had one before."

"Excuse me," said Sidney, raising his hand. "But isn't Tony's about one block away from the school we're supposed to be in?"

"Yes," said Jeffrey.

"Shouldn't we be concerned about that?"

"Why?"

"Because. What are we doing going to a place where anybody at school could look out a window and see us?"

Jeffrey shrugged. "I don't know."

"Well, could we think about that for a minute?"

"No."

"Why not?"

"Because that's where Grandpa wants to take us."

"So what?"

"So that's where we're going."

Sidney looked hard into Jeffrey's eyes, as if he was searching for something. "Have you lost your mind?"

"No."

"Then why are you talking like this? Why are you just blindly going along with something your grandpa wants to do, even though it could lead to big trouble for every one of us?"

Jeffrey returned Sidney's look. "Because this is not for you, Sidney, and it's not for Charlie, and it's not for me. We're doing this for my grandpa, and if he wants to take us to Tony's, then that's where we'll go. He woke up this morning practically crying, he was so worried about my grandma, and he asked me for a favor, which is something he's never done his entire life. So yeah, I get what you're saying, but it doesn't matter."

Jeffrey sat back in his chair and took a couple of deep breaths to calm down. The last few days hadn't been easy for him. Every night since she had left, his mother had phoned home with an update, and although Grandma Anderson had come through the surgery in relatively fine form, there was talk by at least two of the doctors that the recovery was taking a different route than expected. Exactly what that meant, Jeffrey didn't know, but he was convinced that neither his mother nor his grandfather knew either. He was pretty sure they weren't keeping anything from him, like that his grandma was really about to die or anything like that, but even the people who had recommended the surgery had talked about the risks involved with operating on an eighty-five year old.

Sidney took in Jeffrey's words, then leaned back in his chair and wondered silently how this little story would go over with Mr. Duncan, the boys' principal at school.

Charlie had none of this on his mind. He had already leapt from the logistics of having lunch at a place so close to school to something far more attractive and appealing than the health of Jeffrey's grandma or the well-being of his grandfather. "You know that new secretary at school, Ms. Morrison?" he said.

No one answered him.

"I met her the other day for the first time. Mr. McPherson sent me down for some time sheets. I guess she works half days and then leaves at lunch. Have you guys ever seen her?"

Jeffrey closed his eyes and continued his attempts to relax. Sidney kept staring into space and tried to ignore Charlie.

"She's pretty hot," said Charlie, nodding his head as if someone was actually listening to him. "I mean, she's not gonna be on "Baywatch" any time soon I don't think. But compared to Mrs. Dunsworth. Holy cow! She's unbelievable. She's my kind of receptionist."

Sidney very slowly started to shake his head.

"I had a little conversation with her in the cafeteria the other day," Charlie continued. "She was buying a salad. I asked her if she was a vegetarian and she said no, she just doesn't like French fries every day. I asked her if she liked East Indian food and she said yes."

Sidney stopped shaking his head and looked at Charlie. "You asked her what?"

"If she liked East Indian food."

"Why would you do that?"

Charlie shrugged. "It's a cultural question. People her age like to eat foods from other countries. I was just being curious. Have you ever eaten East Indian food?"

"Yes."

"How many times?"

"Once."

"Was it good?"

"Yes."

"Well, she thinks so, too."

Sidney thought for a moment. "So you just casually asked her if she liked East Indian food."

"What's wrong with that?"

"Did you ask her who she goes with when she eats it?"

"Yes."

"You did?"

"Yes."

"What'd she say?"

"Her friends. Her sister when she's in town. She has one sister and no brothers. Her parents live in Saskatchewan, so they're probably farmers."

"Did she happen to ask you why you were asking her all these questions?"

"No."

"I sure would have."

"You're a guy."

"I know that."

"Well, guys and girls are different. Girls like those homey kinds of questions. They like it when a guy takes an interest in their family. Guys just like talking about themselves."

Sidney started to frown.

"It's true," said Charlie. "I know all about this stuff. Every weekend for like the past five years, my sister Crystal's had a sleepover. She and her girlfriends lie downstairs and talk nonstop about guys and girls and I listen to them through the heat vent in my bedroom. I've fallen asleep some nights listening to them. I've woken up and my whole cheek has had the pattern of the heat vent stuck to it."

"And is that where you learned about the East Indian food?" said Sidney.

Charlie nodded. "My sister had a friend who fell in love with her student teacher last year. She found out he liked East Indian food so she hung out at this restaurant in the city for like a month, waiting for him to show up."

"And?"

"And she never saw him. Turns out the

guy was lying. He'd never had East Indian food in his life. He just wanted to sound good."

Sidney shook his head again. "So what does that tell you about Ms. Beautiful at the school office?"

"Nothing."

"Why not?"

"Because I asked her some questions to see if she was telling the truth or not."

"Like what?"

"Well, I asked her if she likes frogs' legs."

"You what?"

"I asked her if she likes frogs' legs. It's the only gourmet food I know."

"But frogs' legs have nothing to do with East Indian food."

"Sure they do."

"No, they don't."

"They have frogs in India."

"No, they don't."

"Sure they do. Frogs and cows."

"Well, I know they have cows, but you can't eat them," said Sidney. "They're sacred."

"That leaves the frogs," said Charlie. "That's what I'm saying."

From his place in the chair next to Charlie, Jeffrey opened his eyes. "Do you guys have any idea how stupid you sound?"

"Yes," said Sidney. "But it's not me. It's him."

"It's both of you."

"It's him," said Sidney. "They do not have frogs in India. And even if they did, they don't eat them."

"Well it really doesn't matter anyway," said Charlie. "She said she's never had them before, and that tells me that she wasn't talking about East Indian food just to sound good, because if she was, she'd have said that she's had frogs' legs before and she loved them. But she never said that."

Sidney closed his eyes and rubbed his forehead.

"Well, they don't have frogs' legs at Tony's, Charlie," said Jeffrey. "You can be sure of that."

"They don't have any East Indian food there either," said Charlie.

Sidney contemplated saying something, but decided to save his breath and remain quiet.

Jeffrey turned and looked at the stairs that led from the living room to his grandfather's bedroom and quietly hoped that his grandpa would actually come down fairly soon and not lapse into another nap.

Charlie sat quite happily and thought about Ms. Morrison and wondered what they would talk about the next time they met in the cafeteria.

At 12:30 sharp, the three boys and Grandpa Anderson were led to a booth at the back of Tony's. The waitress handed them each a menu and filled their water glasses.

The restaurant was busy. Sidney scanned the crowd for teachers, but he recognized no one.

"They're probably all at the Legion," said Charlie, with a wink, tipping his hand towards his mouth.

Sidney did not respond. He was feeling very uncomfortable at the moment, and he was letting everyone know it, including Grandpa, who was feeling much better now that he was up and out and not alone.

"What's the matter with you?" Grandpa said after they placed their orders.

"Nothing," said Sidney, looking around again.

"Sure there is. I'd recognize that look anywhere."

"What look?" said Sidney.

"The look on your face. You remind me of a soldier I used to know in the army. Louis Garno. Or was it Alex? I can't remember. There were two of them. Small, little fellas. Always getting into trouble. One of them was eventually discharged for inappropriate behavior. I can't remember what he did. Something. I know that. You don't get discharged from the army for doing nothing. You got put in the kitchen with a potato peeler if you did nothing. Or out by the latrine with a shovel. That's where you found the guys who did nothing. That was the most miserable job on the face of the earth, that one. I never did it myself, but God knows, somebody had to do it, and there were no volunteers. Believe me."

The boys sat quietly as Grandpa spoke.

"Now where was I going with that?" he said, looking around the table.

"Lou Garno," said Jeffrey, who was familiar with his grandpa's occasionally wandering memory.

"Or Alex," said Charlie. "He wasn't sure which one he was talking about."

"Well, I'm pretty sure now it was Alex," said Grandpa, taking a sip of his water. "He was the younger of the two. Always a bit of a hothead. He and I tangled a few times. There was always something under his skin. His brother was no different."

"What about Sidney, Grandpa?" said Jeffrey.

"Who?"

"Sidney."

"There was no Sidney."

"No," said Jeffrey. "I mean Sidney. Right here. You started talking about Sidney and the look on his face."

Grandpa stared at Sidney for a moment. "You look like Lou Garno," he said.

"You told me that already," said Sidney.

"I thought you said it was Alex," said Charlie.

"Alex was Lou's brother," said Grandpa.

"What about him?" said Jeffrey.

"I served with him in the army. Four years. Or was it five?"

"But what about him?" said Jeffrey. "What does he have to do with Sidney?"

Grandpa started to frown.

"You looked at Sidney's face and said you would recognize that look anywhere. And then you mentioned Lou Garno, and you said he had a brother named Alex."

Grandpa nodded. "You look nervous,"

he said to Sidney, as the clarity returned. "Like something bad is about to happen."

"Don't say that," said Sidney. "I happen to think something bad is about to happen, but I would rather it didn't come true."

"That's just like Lou," said Grandpa.

"What about Alex?" said Charlie.

"Alex took a bullet between the eyes during a training drill. He was in the wrong place at the wrong time. And not for the first time, either."

"He took a bullet in the head?" said Jeffrey, stunned by the sudden turn in Grandpa's story.

The old man nodded. "He was never the same after that."

"You mean he lived?" said Jeffrey.

"No. He died right there on the spot."

"So that must mean Lou was the one who was discharged then," said Charlie, in an attempt to keep the facts straight.

Grandpa stopped to think again. "Did I say Lou?"

"No. But if Alex was killed . . ." said Charlie.

"Maybe I've got the wrong family," said Grandpa.

Sidney shook his head and turned to take another look around the restaurant.

"I thought it was those darn Garnos but maybe I'm wrong."

"Well, which one of your friends looked like Sidney?" said Charlie.

Grandpa did some more thinking. "There were always plenty of worried faces where I was located."

Sidney looked from one side of Tony's to the other, then returned his attention to the table.

"It's okay if you can't remember, Grandpa," said Jeffrey. "Sidney's not really like this all the time anyway. He never worries."

Sidney smiled when he heard that and started to relax. When the pizzas came he dug in with the others. He enjoyed the food so much that he didn't even look up when Ms. Morrison popped in to pick up her take-out order.

She looked briefly at Sidney and Jeffrey and did not recognize them. She recognized Charlie immediately. She didn't know why he was in the restaurant, though. She thought about that as she walked back to her car, and made a note to herself to ask about it the next day at school.

8

The boys completed their day of freedom by going home and finally digging into the videos Charlie had lifted from his dad's closet.

They did this after Grandpa Anderson announced that he was too tired to do any more driving and was ready for another nap.

"Sleep tight," Charlie called as Grandpa made his way up the stairs to his room.

Sidney's eyes were wide with excitement. Even Jeffrey seemed ready to see what Charlie had brought.

When they heard the click of the door, the three boys raced downstairs and over to Charlie's collection of luggage. They were as excited as six year olds racing to the tree on Christmas morning.

Charlie held his hands out in a request for patience, then he opened his suitcase and pulled out a mid-sized box with a lock on it. Then he reached into his pocket and pulled out a key.

The videos were all labeled. Charlie took one out and hustled it over to the VCR.

"What's it called?" said Jeffrey.

"Who cares?" said Charlie.

Jeffrey followed Charlie and looked at the case. "That's not a Triple X movie," he said, pointing to the title.

"Sure it is," said Charlie, turning on the television.

"It's a Christmas movie," said Jeffrey. "*It's A Wonderful Life* is the name of a Christmas movie."

Charlie put the tape into the machine. "Have you ever seen it?"

"No, but I've heard about it."

The tape clicked into place, and Charlie, barely able to contain himself, hit the play button. "Well, my friend, I think you're about to find out that when they say it's a wonderful life, they ain't talking about Christmas."

A minute later, the movie began. It was black and white. A boy named George Bailey was playing with his friends.

"What is this?" said Sidney, sitting on the couch.

"It's a Christmas movie," said Jeffrey. "It's about this kid named George Bailey who becomes a man who never gets to do what he wants until some angel shows him that his life is valuable just the way it is. My mom watches this show every Christmas. And she cries every time she watches it. This is not a Triple X movie."

Charlie let it run for another few minutes. As the show moved along, George became a man who got a suitcase as a present.

"This is not a Triple X movie," said Sidney.

"Well wait a minute," said Charlie, still hopeful. "Let the guy get going on his trip. You know how those big cruises go. They get everybody out to the middle of the ocean and then, you know, when nobody on shore is watching, things happen."

"I don't think so, Charlie," said Sidney.

"How else do you think the *Titanic* sank? Everybody was too busy chasing each other around to notice anything."

"But he doesn't go anywhere," said Jeffrey. "That's the whole point of the show."

"Of course he goes somewhere. Look at the suitcase he just got. He's gonna get on a boat and meet some people and things will take off. Just wait."

"No, he doesn't," said Jeffrey.

"I really don't think so," said Sidney.

"Sure he does," said Charlie.

"Black-and-white films aren't like that," said Sidney.

"Maybe it bursts into color as soon as he leaves the dock," said Charlie.

Jeffrey moved to the VCR and pressed the stop button, followed quickly by eject. The tape came out and he passed it to Charlie. "Try another one," he said.

Charlie went back to his suitcase and pulled out another video. "This time we got one," he said, smiling and raising his eyebrows. "It's European."

"What's it called?"

"*Casablanca*."

Jeffrey rolled his eyes. Sidney started to shake his head.

"You guys don't think so?"

"*Casablanca* is not European, you idiot," said Sidney.

Jeffrey started to laugh.

"What is it, then?"

"It's a regular movie," said Sidney. "It's about a guy who runs this bar in some little town where people wait to get back to America from the war. It's not European. It's boring."

Charlie stared in shock at the video in his hands.

"I think you've been duped, Charlie," said Jeffrey.

"I think you're an idiot, Charlie," said Sidney.

"But this is my dad's special collection."

"Well, apparently your dad's not quite the swinger you thought he was," said Sidney.

"But he's always talking about his private collection."

"Maybe that's why he keeps it private: no one else wants to see it."

"And he's always saying things like, 'You better not touch them. They'll burn your fingers they're so hot.'"

"Well, maybe he stole them," said Sidney.

"I think he was probably just joking around," said Jeffrey. "He was tricking you, just like you always do to everyone else."

"Yeah. He was tricking you," said Sidney. "You and your old man, a pair of tricksters just making people laugh wherever you go."

Charlie continued to stare at the video. He had truly thought that he had brought a suitcase full of gold when he arrived at Jeffrey's house, and he was not responding well to the discovery that his father's prize collection was just a bunch of old, colorless movies.

"Well, look at it this way, Charlie," said Sidney. "Instead of having a dad who hides dirty movies in his closet, you have one who saves black-and-white classics. That's not a totally bad thing."

"What about the magazines?" said Jeffrey.

"What magazines?" said Sidney.

"Charlie said he had a bunch of magazines that would make my head spin."

Charlie shook his head. "They're old *Sports Illustrated* magazines. I checked them out already."

"Old *Sports Illustrated* magazines?" said Sidney.

Charlie shrugged. "He likes sports."

"Any swimsuits?"

Charlie shook his head. "Just the Yankees."

The room went quiet.

"For some reason, I wasn't surprised to see those," said Charlie. "But this." He held up the video in his hand. "This is a shocker."

"I think you probably would have been more surprised if they actually were Triple X videos," said Jeffrey.

"I don't know," said Sidney. "His dad's a truck driver, you know. My mom's dated truck drivers before. They can be pretty crazy."

"I think you would have been more surprised," said Jeffrey again.

Charlie said nothing. He was just about to give some serious thought to what it was like to be on the receiving end of a joke or a tall tale, when someone knocked on the front door.

The boys didn't move. Then Jeffrey silently slipped across the room and looked through the window. "It's a guy," he said. "And he's wearing big winter boots. Two of them. One on each foot."

Sidney closed his eyes and tried to remain calm. In his mind he could see the old green-and-white pick-up truck from this morning parked in front of Jeffrey's house, and fresh footsteps in the snow leading from the truck to Jeffrey's front door.

"Well, go answer the door," said Charlie. "Ask him if he wants to buy some videos. Cheap."

Jeffrey began to move towards the stairs.

"No, don't," said Sidney. "Don't answer the door."

"Why not?" said Jeffrey.

"Because I know who it is. It's the guy who chased me over here the other day."

"But this guy has two legs," said Jeffrey.

Sidney took in a deep breath and let it out slowly. "It's his buddy. The other guy's probably sitting in the truck, waiting for him. I saw them this morning, cruising up and down your street. That's what I was looking at through your window."

Jeffrey stood without moving and stared at Sidney. "So this is the friend of the guy you punched in the face?"

Sidney nodded. "I think so."

"You mean, the one-legged guy he punched in the face," said Charlie, to clarify.

Jeffrey started to turn pink.

"And now he's come to get his revenge," Charlie added.

Sidney nodded again. "That would be my guess."

Charlie glanced over at Jeffrey, then back at Sidney. "So what are we gonna do?"

Sidney returned Charlie's stare for a

moment, then he looked down at the carpet. He was still not in the mood for a battle, which was unusual for him.

"For some reason, I just don't feel like fighting right now," he said. "After last night, talking about my dad and everything, I don't know. I just don't feel like getting into anything. I don't feel mad enough."

Charlie hesitated before speaking. "Well, that's real nice," he said. "It's nice to hear that. But it doesn't exactly take care of the problem."

The person outside pounded on the door again.

"I'm sorry," said Sidney helplessly, lifting his hands in the air and letting them drop on the couch.

"So am I," said Charlie.

"Well we can't just wait for him to leave," said Jeffrey. "If Grandpa wakes up and hears all this going on, he's gonna be really mad."

Charlie turned his head towards the ceiling and thought. This was not what he had hoped to be doing when Grandpa Anderson announced that he was going to bed. He was also not especially pleased that he seemed to be the one who had to deal with Sidney's visitor without Sidney's help.

"I could just go up and tell him you're not here," said Jeffrey. "I mean, if you're not here, you're not here, right? The guy can't come through the house looking for you. He's not the police or anything."

Sidney nodded without enthusiasm. Jeffrey's idea might get rid of his pursuer for now, but not forever, and they all knew that Jeffrey was by far the worst liar of the group.

"Or would that work?" said Jeffrey, upon brief reflection.

Sidney shook his head.

"That leaves me then, doesn't it," said Charlie.

Sidney and Jeffrey nodded.

"Mr. Trickster," said Charlie, out loud, but to himself.

"Mr. Trickster Jr.," said Sidney. "Don't forget your roots."

Charlie gave him a look. Then the person upstairs pounded on the door again.

"Go do your thing," said Sidney. "But don't get carried away with it. Your back-up is taking the night off."

Charlie took a deep breath to collect himself.

"Go to it, Charlie," said Jeffrey, looking nervous.

Charlie gave his friends a final look and turned towards the stairs.

Charlie opened the front door. Before him stood a man with sandy brown hair swept to one side, and a dark, furry mustache. He was slightly built and had beady brown eyes that twitched constantly, as if he, rather than Charlie, was the anxious one.

"Hello," said Charlie, opening the door about six inches.

The man did not move and said nothing. He looked startled.

"Can I help you?"

"Who are you?" the man finally said.

"I'm Charlie. Who are you?"

"I'm Richard Stewart."

Charlie did not make the connection between Richard and Jeffrey.

"You're here to see Sidney, I assume?" he said instead, taking the direct approach.

Richard frowned. "Who?"

"Sidney. The guy you're looking for. He's downstairs getting ready."

The crease in Richard's forehead grew deeper. "I'm not—"

"He said to tell you to scram and never come back or he'll round up his pals from karate and teach you a lesson you'll never forget."

Richard Stewart stared closely at Charlie for a moment and said nothing.

"He said no woman he knows is gonna get treated like that. Not by you or anyone else."

Richard's face began to flush. He swallowed hard and struggled for something to say. He had known that coming to the house would not be easy, not after leaving Jeffrey and Elizabeth the way he had, but he had not expected anything as confrontational as this, especially from some stranger.

"Now get off my property," said Charlie, as a finale.

Dumbfounded, and feeling like a rat, Richard took a step back. Then he stopped. "Your what?"

"You heard me."

"But this is not your property."

"Oh no?"

"It can't be. Sam and Edna Anderson live here."

"So?"

"So, how can you say it's your property?"

Charlie hesitated. The laws of land titles and property ownership were not exactly his specialty. But he did have a hunch.

"They're my grandparents," he said. "What belongs to them belongs to me. I've seen their wills."

Pure confusion appeared on Richard Stewart's face. "They're your what?"

"You heard me. They're my grandparents."

Richard took a step back towards the door. "What did you say your name was again?"

"Charlie."

"Charlie what?"

"That's all you need to know."

"Who else lives in this house, Charlie?"

"None of your business."

Richard stood and stared for a moment. "Do you know who I am?"

"No."

"I'm Jeffrey Stewart's father."

Charlie's heart leapt as if he had just been introduced to the Grim Reaper.

"Now I don't know who this Sidney person is that I'm supposedly looking for."

Charlie licked his lips to talk.

"And I cannot say I'm looking forward to meeting him."

Charlie opened his mouth to explain, but no words came out.

"But I would like to step inside for a moment and pass on my condolences to my father-in-law. And to find out how Jeffrey's doing."

Charlie's eyebrows shot up his forehead like twin arrows. "Grandma Anderson is dead?"

Richard frowned again. "You didn't know that?"

"We've been out all day."

"There were no messages?"

Charlie shrugged. "I guess not. Nobody said anything." He pushed the door open and let Jeffrey's father step inside.

"That's odd," said Richard.

"I'll be right back," said Charlie.

He dashed downstairs to get Jeffrey.

The three boys arrived back in the living room together.

"Dad?" said Jeffrey, in disbelief. Charlie had just said that there was someone upstairs to see him, and he had not had the time, nor the inclination, to say who it was and why.

Jeffrey's father put his hands out in front of him, as if to keep his son back. "I've just come to pass on my condolences, Jeff."

Jeffrey stopped in his tracks. "Your what?"

"For Grandma."

"She's dead?"

"I'm afraid so."

"Oh, God."

"She put up a good fight."

Jeffrey was stunned. "How do you know?"

"I got a call from Mabel Forrester. I left work and drove three hours to get here."

"Mabel from up the street?"

"Yes."

"How did she know?"

Richard shook his head. "I don't know. But she did. She'd heard."

Jeffrey felt as if his body was on fire.

"Why would your mom phone a neighbor instead of us?" said Charlie.

Jeffrey shook his head. He was too shocked to think about it.

"Why wouldn't she be phoning us right now?" said Charlie.

Jeffrey's face began to quiver and his eyes

filled with tears. He looked at his father, who only at that moment extended his arms to give his son a hug. Jeffrey moved forward and the two embraced.

Sidney stood back, silent. Charlie continued to think.

"I don't get it," he said. "Why would his mom phone a neighbor instead of us?"

Sidney shook his head.

"She had a good life," said Richard, as he rubbed Jeffrey's back. "She did a lot of things. Made a lot of friends."

From upstairs, the boys heard the sound of a door opening. Jeffrey continued to sob quietly in his father's arms. Charlie stopped talking and Sidney looked to the staircase and gulped. This was not going to be an easy time for Grandpa.

A moment later, the old man appeared on the stairs.

"What's all the racket about?" he said, sounding like he had just woken up. "I leave my hearing aid on for the first time in my life, and I can't sleep it's so noisy." He walked slowly down the remaining stairs. "What's the matter with him?" he said, pointing to Jeffrey. Then he saw Richard. "What are you doing here?"

"I have bad news, Dad," said Richard.

"What is it?"

"Mom died this afternoon. Mabel Forrester called and told me."

"She did?"

"Yes."

"Well, I talked to Grandma before I went to bed. About an hour ago. She's feeling fine. She ate her first full meal since the surgery."

Richard's mouth fell straight open. Jeffrey stopped crying and turned to hear his grandpa.

"So go tell Mabel she got it wrong again. The last time she called here she said Ian Funstad was dead. I said Ian Funstad died twenty years ago. She said this was his son. I said he didn't have a son. She said it was his son-in-law then. I said he didn't have any son-in-laws. With daughters that looked like his, it's a wonder they could hang on to their pets."

Grandpa Anderson walked past the group in the doorway and slowly made his way towards the kitchen. Then he stopped and turned around. "Any of you boys know how to make tea?"

Sidney said yes, and they all trooped into the kitchen.

9

Sidney put on a pot of tea. Charlie got out five cups and saucers and put them around the table.

Jeffrey sat next to his dad, but they were not talking any more, or hugging.

Grandpa sat at his usual spot, at the end of the table near the telephone.

When the tea was ready, Sidney took the pot over to the table, then went back for the cream and sugar.

"This is good," said Jeffrey, after taking a sip.

Sidney nodded. He made tea every night at home, and his mother's standards were as high as the Queen's, so he was not surprised that people liked it.

"I find it a bit strong," said Charlie, setting down his cup.

"Add some sugar," said Sidney.

"I can't. It goes right to my waist."

"Then add water."

"That'll just make it cold."

Sidney stared hard, but said nothing.

"Tea is like beer for me," said Charlie, a moment later. "I have one cup and I have to pee three times. It's crazy."

"Like beer?" said Richard, looking at Charlie and then at Jeffrey. Jeffrey shrugged and shook his head.

"It is," said Charlie.

"When have you had beer before?" said Sidney.

"I've had beer lots of times."

"When?"

"Football games. Hockey games."

"You have not."

"Me and the boys up in the bleachers. We go crazy."

"You've never had a beer in your life."

"All right," said Charlie, with a shrug. "So what? So I've never had beer before. My mom uses that line every time she has a cup of tea and it always gets a laugh."

"It's probably a different crowd," said Jeffrey, noting the tension in the room.

Charlie took another sip of tea and put his cup down. "Thanks again for the pizza this afternoon, Grandpa Anderson," he said, changing the subject.

Grandpa nodded but said nothing. He was a million miles away.

"You kids went out for pizza at lunch?" said Richard, grateful for the opportunity to say something that had nothing to do with anything important, or so he thought.

Jeffrey nodded and hoped like crazy that Charlie would shut his mouth and not say anything more about their day.

"We did more than that," said Charlie anyway. "We took the whole day off."

Richard raised his eyebrows. "You what?"

"We took the whole day off. No school in the morning. No school in the afternoon."

Jeffrey took in a deep breath and shot a quick look across the table at Charlie. "Grandpa asked us to skip school today," he said to his dad. "He said he was lonely and he wanted our company. So we went with him."

Richard Stewart thought about that for a moment. As an estranged father who had abandoned his wife and child without giving them a moment's notice, he was well aware of his lack of rights when it came to discipline. But at the same time, he did not feel quite right just sitting there saying nothing. "Did you talk with anyone at school about this?" he said finally.

Jeffrey, Sidney and Charlie all looked at him at once. At first, their expressions were blank, as if he had just spoken in a foreign language. Then Charlie frowned. "You mean, did we ask if we could skip?"

"Well, no. Not exactly," said Richard. "Did you phone someone and explain your situation? Did you tell your teachers that you wouldn't be at school today?"

The three boys were silent. The idea of running their good deed by anyone at school had come no closer to crossing their minds than a comet falling from the sky comes to running into Tony's Pizza Place.

Still, Charlie looked reflective for a moment and nodded. "I thought about doing that," he said.

"You did not," said Sidney.

"Sure I did. That's what got me thinking about Ms. Morrison. She probably would have answered the phone."

"Get lost," said Sidney.

"I'm serious. Then I could have cleared up that business about the frogs' legs. She would have known for sure."

"I don't think so, Charlie," said Jeffrey, shaking his head.

"She eats East Indian food all the time. Of course she would have known."

"I don't mean about that," said Jeffrey. "I mean, I don't think you ever thought of phoning the school."

"Sure I did."

"Well, you kept it a secret."

"You kept cutting me off, every time I opened my mouth."

"I wish," said Jeffrey.

Grandpa Anderson cleared his throat and stopped the conversation before it could go anywhere else. "I've been hearing this cackling day in and day out between you boys," he said, his voice deep and gruff. "You sound like a family of birds fighting over a worm. At first I switched my hearing aid off so I wouldn't have to listen to it. Then I realized what it was about. Friendship. You boys getting along with each other. This is the way you communicate. And lately, I've started hearing something else. Loyalty. To each other, and to me. That's what today was all about."

The three boys exchanged looks but didn't speak.

"That's what you don't get," continued Grandpa, turning his attention to Richard. "You don't understand that part of it. That's why you asked such a stupid question."

Richard's face went red. He knew the old man had been leading to something, and in a way, he was relieved that it was finally out on the table.

"I understand loyalty," he said, his hands starting to shake.

Jeffrey's father was not exactly a lord of the ring in the area of confrontation. When it came to swapping words with Grandpa Anderson, he seldom had enough wind to snuff out a candle, much less fuel a long, emotional debate.

"Oh, you do?" said Grandpa Anderson, warming up.

"I like to think so."

"Is that why you left your wife and son the way you did? Out of loyalty?"

Richard took a moment to wipe his forehead with his hand, which was already wet with sweat. This was neither the time nor the place to explain the actions he had taken several months ago, but he was not sure whether he had a choice any more.

"I'm not saying I'm perfect," he said, by way of skirting the issue.

"You're not?" said Grandpa.

Richard shook his head. "That's the last thing I'm saying."

"Well, that's the last thing I'd ever think."

The shaking of Richard's hands became noticeable to the boys, just as it did to customers of his who drove harder and harder for better deals at the furniture store. Richard would eventually have to call in Tommy, his twenty-four-year-old supervisor, to close the deal, and later, in the staff room or outside in the parking lot at the end of the day, Tommy and the other salespeople would make jokes about him. "No. That's not what I'm saying at all. Maybe my definition of loyalty is just different from yours."

"Well, let's hear it," said Grandpa.

Richard licked his lips. He knew without a doubt that this would have been easier to deal with had Grandma Anderson actually died. Not because he disliked her, but because he knew he could handle the grief. Tears were not a problem for him, not even his own son's, in a situation like that. But the idea of dropping the gloves with Grandpa held less appeal than unloading the furniture truck on Monday mornings with Morley, the near-sighted, dim-witted stockroom clerk who chewed garlic sausage like gum and horked wads of phlegm all over the loading ramp.

"Well ... I ... " he said, failing to burst out of the blocks the way he had hoped. He took another crack at it, as he had practiced with his therapist, and got it out. "I needed to fulfill my loyalty to myself," he said. "I needed to take care of me."

Grandpa Anderson leaned forward on the table. His frown was so deep his face was practically folded in two. "You what?"

"I had to take care of me," said Richard, staring almost directly down. "I was being taken over by you, by my mother-in-law, by my wife and by my son. I had no idea who I was any more, or what I was. And I had to find that out. I have to find that out. I'm still looking."

"In a furniture store?" said Charlie, who could not help himself.

"I also have to eat," said Richard.

Grandpa Anderson sat back in his chair. "That is what I mean by loyalty to myself," said Richard. "And I'm very sorry it went this way. But it's not all my fault."

Grandpa said nothing. Jeffrey sat frozen in his chair and did not even bother to try and make sense of what his father was saying. Charlie sipped his tea and followed the lead of the others. Sidney had heard this hapless spiel before, not from his own dad because he was too young to recall how that departure had gone, but from many of the men his mother had dated since then.

It was Grandpa who spoke first. "You'd make a very poor soldier with that attitude, Richard," he said, solemnly. "And a very poor father. I think you'd better go."

Richard sat for a moment before leaving. He did not feel terrible for what he had said. He was not terrified to see the look in his young son's eyes. But he knew his time with the Anderson family was now officially and completely over, and with that came some remorse, for at one time he had loved every one of them.

He slipped out of his chair and went to put on his shoes. He glanced briefly at Jeffrey but said nothing.

Jeffrey considered going to say goodbye,

but he stayed put, knowing that his heart would probably be too heavy or cracked in too many places to get it back into the kitchen.

They all sat and listened as the front door opened and then closed.

Sidney rose and topped up everyone's tea, including Charlie's, without asking.

Then Jeffrey broke the silence. "Well, I guess now we know, don't we?" He looked around the table. "Now we know why my dear old dad ditched us the way he did."

Charlie drummed on the table with his fingers. It was the only sound in the entire house.

Jeffrey thought for a moment before continuing. "You know what the lousiest part of all this is?" He was staring directly at his teacup. "I mean, I miss my dad and all that, but it's not like we were the closest family on the face of the earth to begin with. But what bugs me most is, ever since I was about three years old, all I've ever wanted was a little brother or sister. Someone to play with and look after. But you know, my mom's gonna come home in a couple of days and we're gonna celebrate her forty-second birthday, and unless some guy comes into her life and absolutely blows her doors off, it's not gonna happen. I'm never gonna get one."

"Your mother used to say that, too," said Grandpa. "But we had her late in our lives, and then your grandma got sick for a few months and we were told 'No more babies,' and that was that. Elizabeth had to wait until you came along, which she did."

Jeffrey nodded. He knew fatherhood was an option, but it was a very long way off, and being a dad seemed a whole lot different than being a big brother to someone.

"Well, for what it's worth, two has always been enough for me," said Sidney, getting into the conversation. "I've never wanted anyone else in my life."

"You don't?" said Jeffrey.

"No way."

"Not me," said Jeffrey. "I look at a family like Charlie's and I think he's the luckiest guy in the world."

"Me?" said Charlie.

Jeffrey nodded.

"You think I'm the luckiest guy in the world?"

"Uh-huh."

"I don't think so, my friend. I have four

sisters at home who drive me nuts every minute of my life. And when they've all gone out someplace, my mom comes at me. And when she's gone out someplace, my dad parks his rig outside my window and starts blowing his horn for a little guy-time. You know what we do together? We go to Canadian Tire and buy auto parts. You know what that's like? I know every cashier in that place by name. I know the shifts of half the people who work there. I know all the other regular customers by heart. I go in there and stand by the televisions while my dad looks for his stupid parts, and I'm like, 'Oh, hello, Roy. How's the new Chevy?' or 'Hello, Mrs. Ronstad. How are the little ones? Cindy-Lou over her cold yet?' It's weird in there. It's like a club with no food and no chairs."

"That's what I mean, though," said Jeffrey. "You have so many things going on in your house. You know what happens here? If Grandpa needs a new part for the car, we all go. Right, Grandpa? It takes us four hours, round trip, from the time he says, 'I need a new part for the car,' to when we all get back in the house. Four hours, and that's staying in town. And when we get home, Grandpa goes upstairs for a nap, Grandma puts her feet up in the living room, and Mom tells me I have to be quiet so I don't wake anybody up. So really, it takes a whole day."

Grandpa nodded in agreement. "It can take a long time."

"And the last time we went, he got the wrong part. The guy gave him a this instead of a that, or some stupid thing, and the whole day was wasted."

"At least it's quiet," said Charlie, looking at the bright side.

Jeffrey shook his head. "Yeah. At least it's quiet. It's quiet in here when everybody's moving. When everybody's sitting still you can hear a pin just lying on the counter. It doesn't even have to drop. You'd hear an echo half the time if a pin dropped in here."

"We don't drop pins in our house," said Sidney. "My mom pokes me with them. Three times last week she jabbed me with one because I was doing something wrong."

"Your mom jabs you with a pin?" said Charlie.

"Not hard, but yes, to get my attention. And she throws high-heeled shoes. She slams doors. She hucks things out the window even though we live on the third floor."

Charlie and Jeffrey exchanged glances.

"See what I mean?" said Sidney. "I don't need another voice in the family to make my life interesting. I got one very loud one already."

"What were you doing wrong to get stuck with a pin?" said Charlie.

Sidney shrugged. "I don't know. I don't remember. Not doing my homework, probably. Mom wants me to start gearing up for high school. She wants me to get into a college so I can learn something and make a good living for myself. So I can live in a house and not some crummy little apartment for the rest of my life."

"You talk to your mom about college?" said Charlie.

"Sometimes that's all we talk about. She's getting very worked up about that. She wants me to have a career chosen by the end of grade nine. She wants me to go to college right after high school. And she wants me out of the apartment before I turn twenty."

"Twenty?" said Charlie.

"At the latest."

"What's the rush?"

"Because you learn more when you're on your own. That's what she says, anyway. She was out of her house when she was fifteen."

"Does your mom talk to you about school?" said Charlie, turning to Jeffrey.

Jeffrey started to nod. "She talks about university. She's saving for my tuition. I told her if I go, I'm going to one away from here."

Charlie frowned. "The only thing my mom ever says to me is 'Leave some food for your sisters.' We never talk about stuff like university or jobs."

"That's because she wants you to leave some food for your sisters," said Sidney. "That's her main concern, right there."

Charlie shook his head. "No. It's because I'm number five in the family, and my mom and dad are burnt out. I can practically do whatever I want and get away with it. That's why my sister Crystal wants to scratch my eyes out every time she sees me. They still care about her."

"Oh, come on," said Jeffrey.

"It's true. They're tired. They tell me that every day. If I don't come up with something spectacular to say, they wouldn't even listen to me half the time."

"Or so you think," said Jeffrey.

"So I know," said Charlie.

"Well, I would still like a big family," said Jeffrey. "But it's not going to happen in this lifetime, unless I make one of my own."

The boys went silent after that. Not because they had run out of things to say, but because it had been a long day.

Grandpa Anderson, who had started to fade as the conversation went on, rose from the table and thanked Sidney for the tea. The boys then gathered all the cups and saucers and took them to the dishwasher.

Then they went downstairs, quietly, to go to bed. There was no more talk of beer or videos or how good the pizza at Tony's was.

And of course, none of them mentioned anything about Ms. Morrison, because none of them had seen her.

10

At 9:15 the following morning, all three boys were called to the principal's office.

Unlike previous visits, Mr. Duncan was waiting for them when they arrived. He closed the door and told them to sit. Then he moved around behind his desk and sat down and smiled.

Mr. Duncan was not the most severe principal in the district. He could not recall the last time he had yelled at a student, and suspensions at his school were lower than at any other by a long shot.

For these reasons, he was viewed as a softy by his staff, a pushover by the superintendent and a problem by the trustees on the school board.

"We're not looking for a prison warden,"

they told him during their last meeting. "But we have to be sure that the message that gets out to our parents is that all students in this school district are treated with equal fairness and firmness, and any violation of the rules will not be tolerated."

"Absolutely," said Mr. Duncan, nodding. "I couldn't agree more."

"No more second chances," added board member Alice Thompson, a retired school-teacher. "Forty-seven years in a classroom and not once did I let a student get away with break-ing a rule."

"I can vouch for that," said Mr. Duncan.

"Oh, I know you can," said Mrs. Thompson. "I remember you very well as a student. I remember you sneezing without cov-ering your nose. Crying whenever it rained. And running from Andrew Taylor when he came at you with a bullfrog. A little tiny bull-frog and you made such a ruckus. And now he's dead after serving for his country and you're sitting here listening to me tell you how to behave again." She shook her head. "Your poor mother," she added, under her breath.

Mr. Duncan looked on as respectfully as he could, and was soon dismissed.

And now this. His three favorite students caught skipping school in a pizza parlor by a part-time secretary who kept nattering about East Indian food as if she had invented it.

He smiled at the boys to calm his nerves. This was a big one for him. There was no doubt in his mind that if he let them off with a warning, the entire school board and every principal and superintendent in the province would hear about it before the school buses pulled out of the parking lot at the end of the day.

And if he suspended them? Well, he would certainly hear about that, too, wouldn't he. There would be a race to his office, and whether the winner was Tizzy Martin or Bella Cairns or Sam Anderson wouldn't matter, either way he would be the loser.

So, he smiled.

"Hello, boys," he said, breaking the ice.

"How do you do, sir," said Charlie.

Sidney and Jeffrey simply nodded.

"How was the pizza yesterday?" He decided to get to the point right away. Charlie could make small talk with a mute, and Mr. Duncan did not want to drag this meeting out any longer than it had to be.

"It was delicious, thank you," said Charlie.

This was the boys' plan, hatched at the speed of sound as they walked down the hallway towards the office: admit everything, deny nothing and plead for forgiveness when the punishment came down.

"Good," said Mr. Duncan.

"How did you know we were having pizza, anyway?" said Charlie, out of curiosity.

Mr. Duncan told them about Ms. Morrison.

Sidney shook his head. Jeffrey's face changed color. Charlie started to glow. "She recognized me?" he said.

"Apparently," said Mr. Duncan. "She said you were with two other boys, and you were all sitting in the restaurant eating pizza when you should have been in school."

"She recognized me," said Charlie again, a dreamy smile spreading across his face.

"What about my grandpa?" said Jeffrey, spotting a hole in Ms. Morrison's story.

"What about your grandpa?" said Mr. Duncan.

"He was with us."

"I beg your pardon?"

"He was with us. That's why we went for pizza. He was sitting in the booth right beside me."

"Ms. Morrison never said anything about your grandpa," said Mr. Duncan.

"Well, he was with us," said Jeffrey. "That's why we went for pizza. He was lonely and he asked us to skip school and then we went for something to eat."

Mr. Duncan sat without speaking.

"Your grandpa was lonely?" he said, finally.

"Yes," said Jeffrey. "So he asked us out for pizza."

"He asked all of you out for pizza?"

"We're living together," said Jeffrey.

"Who is?"

"Charlie, Sidney, me and Grandpa."

"Why?"

"My mom took my grandma to the hospital."

"She what?"

"My mom took my grandma to the hospital."

"What's wrong?"

"She has a heart problem."

"They sliced her open like a baked potato," said Charlie. "They did a neck-to-navel on her. That's what my uncle calls them. He had one ten years ago. He has a zipper running right down the middle of his chest."

Mr. Duncan blanched slightly and looked away.

"A neck to navel?" said Jeffrey, feeling sick.

"That's what he calls it."

"This was minor surgery."

"Not at her age. Nothing's minor when you're over fifty."

Mr. Duncan reached for his water bottle and filled the little glass that his receptionist, Ms. Watson, cleaned and put on his desk every morning as an incentive to drink more. She had also taken to hiding his coffee cup, and keeping any sweets and pastries away until his break in the afternoon. It was a well-known fact that in the past few years, Mr. Duncan had started to put on the bulk, and as Ms. Watson knew, with bulk came cholesterol, and with cholesterol came heart attacks, strokes, and ultimately, a new principal, which she did not look forward to.

"Grandma's going to live, Charlie," said Jeffrey, expressing his truest concern.

Charlie shrugged his shoulders. "Let's hope," he said. "But as you well know, Mr. Duncan, growing old is never easy."

Mr. Duncan put down his water bottle

and took a moment to think. This was not the first time that this threesome had invaded his office and muddled his mind with their repertoire of comments, stories, challenges, and God knows what all else. He was becoming increasingly aware that Ms. Morrison's eyewitness testimony was springing more leaks than a homemade canoe. Nevertheless, the boys had skipped an entire day of school, and for that they should be held accountable and, ideally, punished.

"Yes, I do, Charlie," he said, mindful to show that he took no offence at the boy's comments.

"I didn't mean you personally. I just meant, you've been around. You've seen it happen."

"I certainly have."

"Although, like my mom and dad, the photo albums of you in your glory days are probably getting pushed further and further back in the closet."

Mr. Duncan smiled.

"Man, I saw a picture of my dad the other day and I barely recognized him. He was slim, muscular. Had the dumbest haircut you've ever seen, but still."

"Let's get back to the point," said Mr. Duncan.

"Yes," said Sidney. "Let's get back to the point."

"What do you boys think we should do about this?" said Mr. Duncan. "You've violated one of the golden rules of our school. I appreciate your concern for your grandfather, Jeffrey, but nevertheless, you've done something you know you're not supposed to do."

He surprised even himself when he asked the question, but at the same time, he knew that anything he came up with would be dissected and rearranged into something not even he would recognize.

"How about a stern warning?" said Charlie.

"Not enough."

"How about a stern warning and laps around the pool every Thursday for a month?" said Charlie.

"You didn't skip gym. You skipped everything else, but you didn't skip gym."

"How about we promise we won't do it ever again, and we wait until Grandma Anderson is home so we don't put any more strain on Grandpa," said Sidney.

Mr. Duncan liked that idea the second he heard it.

"In writing," Charlie added. "It means more."

Mr. Duncan liked that idea even better.

"All right. I want you to write a paragraph on the evils of skipping school. Have it on my desk by Monday morning of next week. And when your Grandma returns home, Jeffrey, let me know and we'll continue our discussion then."

The three boys were silent. They had come to the office expecting to be suspended, and therefore hoping that with a little compassion on Mr. Duncan's part, they would get off with maybe a couple of easy hours in the detention room.

"A paragraph?" said Charlie, who was already late with his assignment for Language Arts.

"Three hundred words," said Mr. Duncan. He was delighted with himself for thinking of such a clever idea. "How does that sound?"

The boys thought for a moment. Charlie had the biggest problem with it since writing was not his favorite subject. Sidney didn't mind too much because writing was his favorite. Only Jeffrey said anything. "You mean skipping school in a general way, or skipping school versus taking care of someone you love in a time of need?"

Mr. Duncan looked at the boy and hesitated.

"None of us are immune from getting sick, sir. My grandpa was just asking for a little help."

Mr. Duncan took in a deep breath.

"Look at you. You could get sick. We'd take you out for pizza."

He smiled. Pizza had been one of the first foods to go after his last visit to the doctor.

"In a general way," he said. "And if you would like to relate it to your own experience you can, but only after you acknowledge that it is not a good thing to do."

"Gotcha," said Jeffrey.

The three boys rose to leave.

"We'll see ourselves out," said Charlie. "You sit down and take it easy."

Mr. Duncan nodded and reached again for his water. He wondered briefly if he would ever have grandchildren who would skip school to take care of him.

11

At 3:00, Roy Giffen sat in his pick-up truck across from the schoolyard and kept his eyes on the kids cutting across the field while his buddy Fritz hobbled into the store for some smokes.

It was a funny sort of arrangement, Roy had to admit, since he wasn't completely sure what the kid he was looking for actually looked like, but Fritz, the brains of the operation, had insisted.

"You stay here," Fritz had said, reaching into the back of the truck for his crutches.

"All right," said Roy above the music he was playing on the cassette player he had just bought for next-to-nothing.

Fritz came out of the store a few minutes later. He crutched his way over to the truck and opened the passenger door just as Roy turned up the volume on his favorite song.

Fritz said something, but Roy didn't hear him. Fritz repeated himself, but Roy went on drumming his fingers on the steering wheel, and when the guitar solo kicked in, Roy buried his head and played along with it on his imaginary guitar like a demon.

Then, quite suddenly, the music stopped.

Roy looked up.

"I said, 'Did you see him?'" said Fritz.

"That's my song, man," said Roy, looking hurt.

"We're not here to listen to music. We're here to find the kid who punched me in the face. Now did you see him?"

Roy started the truck and stuck it in reverse. "No, I didn't."

"How do you know?"

Roy looked over his shoulder and started to back out of the store's parking lot. "What do you mean, how do I know? Do you see the kid sitting here? Do you see me running after some kid across the field over there? No. So I didn't see him."

Fritz waited a moment. "You don't know what the kid looks like, Roy."

Roy stopped the truck. "What?"

"You don't know what the kid looks like."

"So?"

"So how do you know if you've seen him or not?"

Roy frowned.

"How do you know if you've seen him or not if you don't know what he looks like?"

"Well, what are you doing leaving me to look for a kid I don't even know?"

"It was a test," said Fritz, tearing the wrap off the cigarettes.

"A what?"

"A test. To see if you're thinking today."

"I'm thinking today," said Roy, taking his foot off the brake.

"No, you're not."

"I am so."

"No, you're not!"

"I am so!"

"And stop saying you have a song. Guys don't have songs. That bugs me."

"They do so."

"No, they don't. You can say you like that song. Or that this is a great song. But don't say, 'This is my song.' You sound like a fruitcake."

Roy stopped the truck just before he was

out of the parking lot. "This is my truck, Fritz," he said, knocking his finger on the dashboard. "And that is my cassette player with my cassette in it. And if I wanna say that a song I like is my song, then I'm gonna."

Fritz put a cigarette in his mouth and said nothing.

"You start showing a little respect around here. And stop giving me those stupid tests."

Fritz shook his head. "I need you to be thinking today, Roy. For four days we've been trying to find that kid and today's the day I'm gonna do it."

"Well, maybe it is and maybe it isn't. But don't go asking me to look for a kid and then get after me for not seeing him because I don't know what he looks like."

"That's not what I'm mad about."

"Well what is it, then?"

"I'm mad because you said you didn't see him even though you have no way of knowing whether you saw him or not because you don't know what he looks like."

Roy shook his head and turned the truck onto the street.

"So just calm down," said Fritz, looking out his window.

"That sounds like a very stupid test to me," said Roy.

"Well, you failed it. Not me."

"Well, it was your test. How are you supposed to fail your own test? How stupid would that be?"

Fritz stayed quiet and looked out his window as Roy stopped at a traffic light beside the school. Then, just as the light turned green, Fritz said, "There he is, right there."

Roy turned his head to see who Fritz was talking about. "Which one?"

"That kid right there."

"That little guy?"

"That kid with the brush-cut there. Beside that fat kid and the other kid. That's him."

Roy took another look, then sped up to cut the boys off at the next intersection. "Huh, I was right after all," he said.

Fritz turned to look at him. "Right about what?"

"I told you I hadn't seen the kid and I hadn't. I've never seen that kid before in my life."

Fritz shook his head and returned to looking out his window.

"I passed your stupid test after all," said Roy as he drove his truck.

By the time Sidney saw them, it was too late to do anything. The old green-and-white pick-up, which was actually more rust than anything else, pulled in front of the boys just as they were about to turn towards the ravine.

Sidney stopped in his tracks and watched as Fritz stumbled out of the truck and nearly fell trying to pull his crutches out of the back.

Sidney saw Roy step around the front of the truck and stand there with a cigarette hanging from his mouth like he was a cowboy in an old western who had forgotten his matches.

Neither of the two were the biggest people Sidney had ever taken on. Fritz was short and slightly built. He had a small pile of fuzzy hair on his head and a goatee on his chin that, in Sidney's opinion, looked ridiculous. Roy was taller and thicker and wore a jean jacket that left him shivering in the cold. His hands were big though, and Sidney could tell just by looking at him that he knew what combat was about.

Charlie and Jeffrey did not know what was going on until they saw Fritz with the crutches under his arms. As he moved closer to them, they also saw a small mark under his right eye where Sidney had popped him.

Fritz spoke first. "Well, well," he said, with a little smile.

"Well, well, what?" said Sidney.

"Well, well, what have we here?" said Fritz, still smiling.

"We've been looking for you," said Roy, stepping forward.

Charlie and Jeffrey huddled closer to Sidney. This was not a confrontation they were looking forward to.

"Punched anyone in the face today?" said Fritz.

"Not yet," said Sidney. He had his game face on. Any problem he had about getting up for a fight had just disappeared.

"You haven't met Roy before," said Fritz, his eyes on Sidney. "He wasn't with me the day you sucker punched me. His little brother was driving me around."

"You mean the day you hassled my mom," said Sidney.

"You never said you hassled anyone's mom," said Roy, standing beside Fritz.

"I didn't hassle nobody's mom. I stepped out of the truck and this punk belted me before I could get my crutches under my arms."

"What were you doing at my mom's apartment then?" said Sidney.

"I didn't know she lived there."

"You followed her home, you bozo. Of course you knew she lived there."

Roy spoke to Fritz again. "It sounds like you hassled this guy's mom."

"I did not."

"You never said nothing about that before."

"He's lying. I don't even know who his mom is."

"Who's your mom, kid?" said Roy.

"Tizzy Martin. She's a waitress at Kelly's. And you do so know who she is," said Sidney, looking directly at Fritz.

Roy's eyes popped out of his head. "You mean that lady with the frizzy brown hair?"

"Yes," said Sidney.

"And the locket she always wears around her neck?"

"I bought her that for Christmas two years ago."

Roy was stunned. "That's your mother?"

"Yes."

"She's your old lady?"

"Yes."

"So you must be Lindsay, then."

"No, I'm Sidney."

Roy frowned. "I thought she said her son's name was Lindsay."

Sidney shook his head.

"Well, who's Lindsay then?"

"I don't know. There is no Lindsay. Only me, and I'm Sidney."

"You sure?"

"Positive."

Roy stared at his feet for a moment. "Maybe she did say Sidney." Then he looked up again and stepped forward. "Well, it's nice to meet you, Sidney. I like your mother a lot. She's very nice to me whenever I go to Kelly's." They shook hands.

"I'll tell her we met," said Sidney.

"You do that. You tell her I can't wait for another piece of that delicious pie she makes."

"She's not the cook, you idiot," said Fritz, who was getting angrier by the minute watching Roy and Sidney become friends.

"I know that," said Roy. "But she serves it so I call it her pie. She recommends it every time I go in there."

Fritz shook his head. "Look, Roy. This is the kid who punched me in the eye. This is the kid who caused so much trouble the other night that you missed out on a chance to see Sarah because I was too busy putting ice cubes on my face to call to see if she would go out with you or not."

Roy looked back at Sidney. "You know someone named Sarah Waters?"

Sidney shook his head.

"She's someone I love," said Roy.

"I know her," said Charlie, stepping forward.

Roy looked at Charlie. He gave him the once-over. "Who are you?"

Charlie introduced himself.

"How do you know Sarah?"

"She's friends with my sister."

"Who's your sister?"

"Crystal Cairns."

Roy took a step backwards. "Your sister's Crystal Cairns?"

"You bet."

"I don't believe it."

"She talks to Sarah every day. They're best friends."

"I know."

"Sarah's over at our house, like, three days a week."

"No way."

"And every weekend."

"That's incredible."

"Oh, yeah. My mom calls her her fifth daughter."

Roy thought for a moment. "Have you ever heard her talk about me?"

Charlie hesitated. "It's Roy, right?"

"Roy Giffen."

Charlie started to nod. "You know what? I think she was talking about you the last time she was over."

Roy's eyes sprang wide like a rose in full bloom. "She was?"

"I'm positive. Now that I think of it. She was talking about you a lot. And in a pretty nice way, too, if you know what I mean."

Roy was glowing.

"I mean, I couldn't tell you exactly what she was saying, but they weren't laughing or making gagging noises or anything like that."

"Could you do me a favor?" said Roy.

Charlie smiled. "Sure."

"Could you put in a good word for me, the next time she comes over?"

"Absolutely."

"Maybe you could even ask if she'd like to go out with me."

Charlie shrugged. "Why not? Maybe I could even give you a call and you could come over."

Roy's mouth fell open. "You'd do that?"

"Of course."

Roy shook his head. "What a great bunch of guys you are."

Fritz stood beside him fuming. "Do you have any idea why we're here, Roy?"

Roy looked at his friend.

"Do you have any recollection at all of what we're supposed to be doing?"

Roy started to think.

"You're supposed to be hanging a licking on this kid here for hurting your best pal the way he did. Look what he did to me, Roy. I could've been blinded. I could have lost my retina. Like Sugar Ray Leonard. My retina could have fallen off. Remember how upset you were when that happened to him? Well, the same thing could have happened to me."

Roy stared at Fritz.

"Roy here would like to be a champion boxer someday," said Fritz, turning to the boys. "And he's gonna make it. You should see him go. But the day Sugar Ray Leonard lost his retina, that was a long day in this man's life.

And he re-lived that experience when you hit me in the face."

Roy nodded in agreement. Sidney prepared once again to do battle.

Charlie, however, had a different idea.

"Wait a minute, guys," he said.

"For what?" said Fritz.

"I just wanna ask Roy something."

"What?" said Fritz.

Charlie hesitated. He had no idea what he wanted to ask Roy, but he thought he better come up with something quickly.

"How old are you?" he said.

"What difference does it make?" said Fritz.

"I'm seventeen," said Roy.

Charlie looked at Sidney. All of a sudden, he was glad he asked. "I thought you said these guys were twenty-five?"

Sidney shrugged. "I thought they were."

"You thought I was twenty-five?" said Fritz.

Sidney shrugged again.

"You look twenty-five to me," said Charlie, turning it on.

"I do?"

"Sure. With that little thing on your chin. I'd say twenty-five easily."

Fritz looked impressed. "I just grew this

not too long ago."

"It makes you look like a movie star," said Charlie.

"Really?"

Charlie nodded. "Like Johnny Depp or Brad Pitt. Someone like that."

"Brad Pitt?" said Fritz.

"You like Brad Pitt," said Roy.

"I'll tell you who likes Brad Pitt," said Charlie. "My sister Crystal. She loves Brad Pitt."

Fritz hesitated. He looked at Charlie and Charlie could see, quite plainly, what Fritz was thinking.

"She's a huge fan of his."

"Would she like to go out with him?" said Fritz.

"Oh, she'd die," said Charlie. "Right here on the spot. She'd pass out and that would be the end of her."

Fritz thought for a moment, then he started talking. "You know what?" he said, motioning towards Charlie. "When your sister and Sarah are over at your place talking, have you ever heard them say anything about a guy named Fritz?"

Charlie had a feeling this might happen. "Fritz?" he said. "You know what? I know for sure I've heard them talk about that guy who hangs out with Roy all the time."

"They have?" said Fritz.

"I wonder if that could be Mel," said Roy. "I got a buddy named Mel, too, as well as Fritz."

"Mel?" said Charlie, narrowing his eyes. "Mel."

"He's a little fat guy who wears a hood all the time," said Roy.

Charlie shook his head. "No, it's not Mel. They've never said anything about a guy with a hood."

"Not even that they don't like him?" said Fritz hopefully.

Charlie started to nod. "Maybe they've said that. Maybe they have said something about not liking Mel."

"I could live with that," said Roy, looking at Fritz. "I could go out with someone who doesn't like Mel."

"I prefer people who don't like Mel," said Fritz.

They both started to nod.

"Well, how about this?" said Charlie. "Why don't I go home and put in a good word for both of you, and maybe all four of you could double up and go on a date together?

How does that sound?"

"That would be awesome," said Fritz.

"I would really appreciate that," said Roy.

"Consider it done," said Charlie. "I'm really glad we met."

"Hey, me too," said Fritz, extending his hand to Charlie, and then to Jeffrey, who had remained silent.

"Tell your mom I'm sorry I hassled her," said Fritz, to Sidney. "I don't know what I was doing, but I probably got what I deserved."

"Sidney's sorry, too," said Charlie, before Sidney could open his mouth and possibly say something that would reverse the flow of the conversation. "He's talked about you a lot these past few days. He's been very reflective."

Fritz looked at Sidney. "No hard feelings?" he said, extending his hand.

"No hard feelings," said Charlie, taking up Fritz's offer. Sidney remained quiet, but at least he didn't take a swing at anybody.

"You guys need a ride anywhere?" said Roy.

"That's all right," said Charlie. "We're just cutting through here."

"Well, we'll see you around then," said Roy.

"You take care of that leg," said Charlie, to Fritz.

Fritz waved in return and hopped into the truck. Music blaring, the two of them drove off. Roy's head was bobbing to the beat of the tune, and Fritz, whose face was turned to the window again, was smiling, as if he suddenly had a song now, too.

The boys made their way home after dealing with Fritz and Roy and were told by Grandpa that Grandma would be coming home in the morning.

12

The boys were happy, especially Jeffrey, but nothing they said or did could match the excitement and relief in Grandpa's eyes. He gave Jeffrey a hug and slapped Charlie and Sidney on the back. Then he led them into the kitchen for their big surprise.

On the kitchen table there was a big bowl of potato chips and three empty glasses.

Grandpa stood beside the boys as they took the scene in, then he slipped away and opened up the fridge.

Charlie was just about to ask a question when Grandpa cut him off. "We're having a toast, my boys."

He put a can of beer down on the table and looked at them and smiled. Then he cracked the beer, poured about an inch into each of the glasses and saved the rest for himself.

He held the can of beer in the air and said, "To men."

The boys responded immediately. With great excitement, they each picked up a glass and held it up to Grandpa's can.

"To men," repeated Charlie.

"To fighting men," said Sidney, whose adrenaline was still running pretty high.

Jeffrey remained quiet.

"And to women," said Grandpa, continuing with the toast.

"God love 'em," said Charlie.

"To fighting women," said Sidney, thinking of his mother.

"And to boys," said Grandpa, wrapping things up.

"Without them, we wouldn't be here," said Charlie.

"To fighting boys," said Sidney, starting to glow.

"How about to grandpas?" said Jeffrey, turning pink. He had never given a toast before.

"Hey, that's a good one," said Charlie. "To grandpas."

"To this grandpa," said Sidney.

"To all of us," said Charlie.

They touched glasses all around and then swigged back their drinks. Charlie's eyes nearly sprang out of his head as he swallowed his. Jeffrey almost spit his beer back into his glass. Sidney drained his like it was chocolate milk.

Grandpa looked at them all and nodded.

"You boys deserve that," he said.

"Here, here," said Charlie, his eyes still watering.

"You've been a lot of help to me and I appreciate that."

"Not a problem," said Charlie.

"I hope you don't get into any trouble over anything."

"Not at all," said Charlie, taking a quick glance at the others.

"Now dig in and have yourselves a party," said Grandpa, pointing to the chips. "And later on, maybe we can watch one of those movies you were talking about."

"Um," said Charlie.

Then Grandpa laughed. "Don't worry, boys. I know what you're up to. Those aren't some dumb Christmas movies down there. Just don't go crazy."

"Well, actually—" said Charlie.

"But if you want something real good, I've got some old Charlie Chaplin videos in my closet."

"I love those," said Sidney.

"Those are my favorite," said Jeffrey.

"Well, go on upstairs and get them," said Grandpa.

Jeffrey took off out of the kitchen.

Sidney ran downstairs to get the TV ready and Charlie grabbed the chips and followed him.

Grandpa stood for a moment in the kitchen and took another sip of his beer. There wasn't much left in the can, but he didn't mind, his real bachelor party days had ended a long time ago.

Frog Face and the Three Boys

Don Trembath

Charlie, Jeffrey and Sidney are in the seventh grade
and are spending too much time in the principal's
office. Charlie talks non-stop, Jeffrey is too fright-
ened to talk at all, and Sidney would much rather
let his fists hold up his end of the conversation.
Realizing that detention is not solving the continuing problems, Mr. Duncan enrolls them in karate
lessons.

What begins as punishment slowly becomes
bearable and then a pleasure for the three boys as
they all begin to learn about themselves and how to
get along with others.

In his hilarious first novel for younger readers,
bestselling teen novelist Don Trembath is at the
top of his comic form with this look at some of
the misfits in a small-town school.

"A successful blend of comic and emotional
situations ..." – *Quill & Quire*

★ Shortlisted for the 2001 Silver Birch Award
from the Ontario Library Association

1-55143-165-3; $8.95 CAN/$6.95 USA

One Missing Finger

Don Trembath

All Charlie wanted to do was watch a little TV. But no, he's told to walk the dog, and walk her he does, right into a handful of trouble with a beautiful older girl, her very jealous boyfriend and an elusive pair of red gloves.

Meanwhile, Sidney's fallen for Joey even though her mother wants him to buzz off. And Jeffrey just wants his father back. But would getting his parents back together bring happiness to his life?

One Missing Finger continues the story of the three small-town misfits introduced in *Frog Face and the Three Boys*. Reaching new comedic heights as they stumble further through the jungle of friendship and into the swamp of young love, the three boys realize that as they get older, they need to rely on themselves and trust each other.

Don's teen novels, including *Lefty Carmichael has a Fit* and the Harper Winslow series, have all gone on to become bestsellers. *Frog Face and the Three Boys* has been shortlisted for the Ontario Library Association's Silver Birch Award. Don lives in Edmonton, Alberta.

1-55143-194-7; $8.95 CAN/$6.95 USA

Don Trembath was born in Winnipeg, Manitoba, and moved to Alberta at the age of 14. He graduated from the University of Alberta in 1988, with a B.A. in English.

Don's first novel, *The Tuesday Cafe*, was inspired by six years of work at the Prospects Literacy Association in Edmonton. It was nominated for both the YALSA Best Books for Young Adults and the YALSA Quick Picks for Reluctant Readers lists. It also won the R. Ross Annett Award for Children's Literature and made the ALA's "Popular Paperbacks" 1997 list. The second installment in the Harper Winslow series, *A Fly Named Alfred*, was nominated for the prestigious Mr. Christie's Book Award, followed by *A Beautiful Place on Yonge Street*, which was chosen as a YALSA Popular

Paperback for Young Adults. The most recent Harper Winslow story is *The Popsicle Journal*.

Don has also penned *The Black Belt* series for younger readers. This hilarious collection includes *Frog Face and the Three Boys* (shortlisted for the OLA Silver Birch and for the Manitoba Young Readers Choice Award) and *One Missing Finger*.

Coming soon from Orca Book Publishers!

The Hemingway Tradition
Kristin Butcher

We had the top down on our old LeBaron and the sun was beating on us from a sky that was nothing but blue. It was my mom's turn to drive, so I was stretched out in the passenger seat, watching Saskatchewan slide by and thinking there must be a couple dozen different ways for a guy to kill himself.

Shaw's father, a successful author, has killed himself, and Shaw is determined to prove that he is not following in his father's footsteps.

Kristin Butcher is the author of *The Gramma War* and *Cairo Kelly and the Mann*. This is her first novel in the new Soundings series.